AN *Unfortunate Incident*
AT CASTLE ROCK

ANNIE J. DAHLGREN
AND NEAL P. GRAFFY

COPYRIGHT

El Barbareño Publishing
Santa Barbara, CA

Cover Design by Annie Gallup
Design/Layout by Anna Lafferty, Lafferty Design Plus

Photos courtesy Patrick Denman Collection,
Neal Graffy Archive

Photo of Dibblee (Leadbetter) Mansion
courtesy W. Dibblee Hoyt

ISBN: 978-0-9996486-1-2

NOTE:
This is a work of fiction. Names, characters and incidents are either the product of the author's imagination or are used fictitiously.

THANK YOU

Thank you, Monte Schulz, for your knowledge
and guidance. You have my deepest respect
and gratitude.

Thank you, David & Patty West, for the
reassurance to continue after reading the
earliest draft.

Thank you, Annie Gallup and Anna Lafferty, for
the artful presentation of the story.

Thank you, Neal Graffy, for your lifetime of
knowledge and passion for history.

Thank you, Family and Friends, for the love
and inspiration.

FOREWORD

Due to an absence of nearly 90 years, Castle Rock is not a familiar place name to most Barbareños. But for many generations, Castle Rock was a Santa Barbara landmark second only to the Mission as a tourist attraction. As such, and as early as the 1870s, it was the subject of cabinet card photos and stereo views by pioneer photographers and moving into the early 20th century, hundreds of colorful post cards as well as artists' paintings. It was shown on early maps and charts as Point Castillo, a significant land feature that identified the westerly edge of Santa Barbara from the sea and a point of reference for safe anchorage for wind-driven ships.

The word *castillo* is Spanish, and can signify a castle or just a simple fortification. Qualifying for the latter definition, in the early 1800s, a "V" shaped earthen embankment was created on the land behind the point and fortified with a few cannon, overlooking and in theory, protecting the anchorage off West Beach from invaders. The large rock outcropping that rose above the surf and comprised the point took the fancier translation of castillo and became known as "Castle Rock." For a time, the land now comprising City College's east campus, was the estate of Thomas B. Dibblee which he called *Punta del Castillo*. Following his death it was sold to the Leadbetter family and the names "Dibblee Hill" and Punta del Castillo faded away.

Castle Rock passed away around 1930, it was dynamited during the construction of the breakwater. The twin pillars flanking the entrance to the breakwater are just about where Castle Rock once stood. As for the little fort, the extension of Cabrillo Boulevard past Castillo Street in the early 1940s removed the land where it once stood. The only monument to its existence is Castillo Street, named in 1852 , as it was the street closest to the former fort.

The challenge of keeping the past in context may result in some confusion to the reader when it comes to street names. In 1852 when the streets were laid out, the city limits ended at Mission Street. As the city expanded past Mission Street, the new streets were easily and boringly named First, Second, Third, Fourth, Fifth and Sixth (today they are known as Padre, Los Olivos, Pueblo, Junipero, Quinto and Constance). However, here and there the sharp-eyed pedestrian can still find those original names pressed into the sidewalks. What we now call Cabrillo Boulevard was simply East or West Boulevard in 1909. "Cabrillo" wouldn't be added until 1919. The roads of Hope Ranch, originally laid out by the Pacific Improvement Company, reflected the leaders of that company and its associated interests. Hubbard Avenue (now Las Palmas and Marina) was named for Thomas Hamlin Hubbard, director and vice-president of the Southern Pacific Company. Crocker Avenue (Estrella Drive) perhaps served a dual purpose of honoring Charles Crocker one of the "Big Four" founders of the Central Pacific Railroad (later taking over the Southern Pacific Railroad) as well his son, Charles F. Crocker who had been president, vice-president and director of the SPRR prior to his untimely death at age 42.

Always, the challenge of historical fiction is to keep the past as true as possible while interweaving the fictional narrative. To that end, I find myself guided by Star Trek's Temporal Prime Directive. Our heroine, Leontine Birabent, is not a fictional character, and though her situations and comrades mostly are, they are as real to us as Leontine. It has been uncanny, the number of times where Annie has our heroes in a situation that violates our prime directive and we attempt a different angle or even a rewrite, yet the characters themselves will come up with the resolution or sometimes a new character shows up and resolves the problem.

It is our goal to present you, the reader, with as accurate a picture as possible of Santa Barbara's past. One of the best compliments we received of the first in this series, "A Murder at the Potter Hotel" was "I was so carried away, enjoying walking the streets of Santa Barbara in 1908 I didn't care that anyone got murdered." We hope you too, will find yourself transported back in time to the Santa Barbara of 1909 and an Unfortunate Incident at Castle Rock.

Neal Graffy
Santa Barbara, August 2018

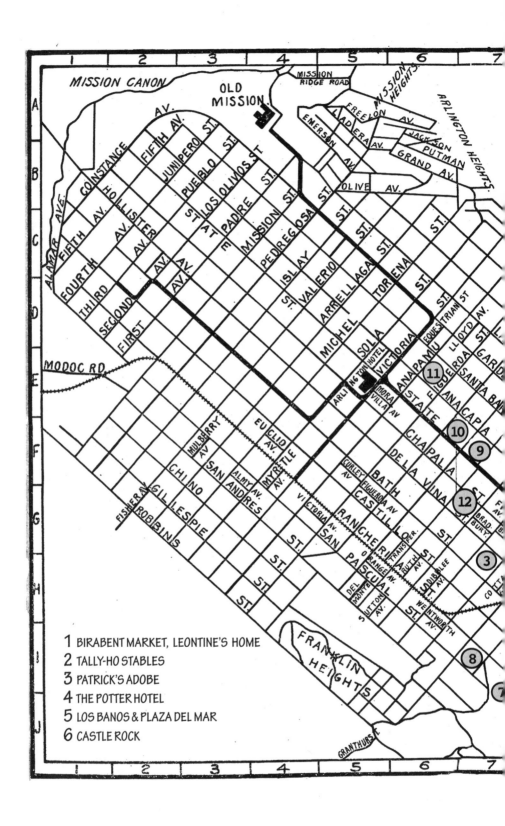

1 BIRABENT MARKET, LEONTINE'S HOME
2 TALLY-HO STABLES
3 PATRICK'S ADOBE
4 THE POTTER HOTEL
5 LOS BANOS & PLAZA DEL MAR
6 CASTLE ROCK

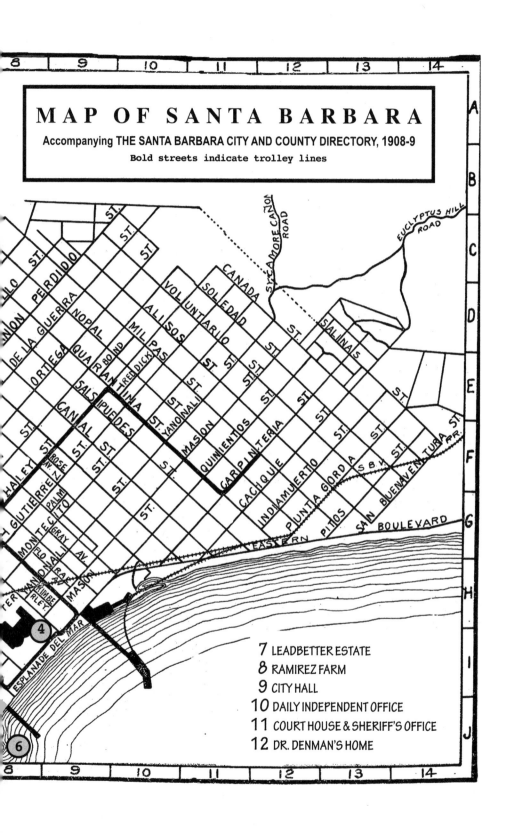

MAP OF SANTA BARBARA

Accompanying **THE SANTA BARBARA CITY AND COUNTY DIRECTORY, 1908-9**

Bold streets indicate trolley lines

7 LEADBETTER ESTATE
8 RAMIREZ FARM
9 CITY HALL
10 DAILY INDEPENDENT OFFICE
11 COURT HOUSE & SHERIFF'S OFFICE
12 DR. DENMAN'S HOME

CHAPTER 1
Friday, August 20, 1909

Coming so early in the morning, the sound of the clanging telephone startled Leontine, and she spilled several drops of tea on her embroidered white linen table covering. Initially, the novelty of having a telephone in one's own home was compelling, and both she and Daisy would leap up with the first chime and offer bright greetings in lyrical tones to whoever was initiating the connection. Fairly rapidly, however, Leontine had become less entranced. She grew increasingly resentful of the thing, elbowing its way into her day unbidden and demanding immediate attention. Moreover, the call was for Daisy in nearly every instance, and when one happy day it occurred to Leontine she could simply ignore it, that is mostly what she did.

She glanced through the kitchen doorway at the mantle clock on the hall table next to the telephone. Not yet eight o'clock. The early hour implied some level of urgency. Leontine rose and moved into the hallway, lifted the receiver, and raised the tulip of the mouthpiece to her chin. "Good morning," she said to the device. "This is Miss Birabent."

"Good morning, Leontine, it's Nicholas Denman," said the tinny voice in her ear.

"Dr. Denman, I trust your day is going well."

"Actually, I was hoping I might trouble you to look after Patrick for a few hours. He's had quite a morning. There's been an unfortunate incident at Castle Rock."

Upon ending the call, Leontine ducked into her bedroom to retrieve her broad-brimmed summer hat and black linen fitted jacket. This morning she had chosen her black-and-white pin-striped walking skirt and a crisp white button-down shirt with broad cuffs and stand-up collar. It would be warm by midday and she would be comfortable, but the morning was still chilly, as August mornings in Santa Barbara so often were, and it was likely to stay that way until the sun managed to burn its way through a thick layer of marine fog that had advanced over the city during the night.

She hurried downstairs to the Birabent Market. Leontine had inherited the market and upstairs residence at 523 State Street upon the untimely death of her father four years earlier. She kept the accounts and ran the store with the help of Remy Birabent, her father's older brother. She passed through the earthy scent of freshly rinsed fruits and vegetables that lay stacked in pyramids on wooden bins at the store's entrance, peeking around shelves stocked with tins, bottles and boxes of merchandise, looking for Uncle Remy to tell him of Dr. Denman's request.

This early on a Friday the market was quiet. She found her uncle on his reading stool at the back of the store completely engrossed in a dime novel. He received the information that Leontine would return with Patrick as soon as possible with a nod and a turn of a page.

On weekdays, the trolley started running when the Mission bells rang at six, and most merchants and workers had already been delivered to their various destinations. The car was sparsely occupied, therefore, when Leontine clambered aboard and handed her five-cent fare to the driver. Her eyes swept the waking businesses along State Street as she worried at the ominous tone in Nicholas Denman's voice. She could feel the stiffness of her smile as she would acknowledge each new rider, and then return a fixed gaze in the direction of the Plaza del Mar on the oceanfront, as if doing so might somehow speed her arrival there.

The trolley rounded the corner onto West Boulevard and the Potter Hotel immediately dominated the view. The immense and luxuriously appointed hotel and its surrounding gardens and walkways rivaled the Pacific Ocean itself in sheer beauty, but Leontine took no notice of the scenery this morning. A block beyond the Potter grounds, the Boulevard ended and the trolley came to a stop in front of the broad Plaza at the foot of Castillo Street.

Plaza del Mar, the adjoining Los Baños del Mar bathhouse, and the nearby Pleasure Pier were the center of Santa Barbara's social life. The Plaza featured wide walkways with several large grass squares framed by outward-facing benches, and a large fountain surrounded by lush vegetation and encircled by a concrete bench. Nestled up against the bluffs rising behind the Plaza was Los Baños del Mar. More than just a "bathhouse", it contained an amusement hall where one could enjoy billiards, ping-pong, bowling and refreshments. For bathing purposes, there was a large indoor heated pool with a second-story gallery for viewing the bathers below, as well as a smaller, quieter pool for women and children and 150 individual bathing rooms with a choice of heated salt or fresh water. Endless quantities of clean, dry towels were supplied by the in-house laundry. On the second floor, a band shell overlooked the Plaza, which was often filled with chairs for Sunday concerts or presentations.

Leontine pulled her jacket closed against the morning air as she stepped from the trolley. She immediately spotted Patrick and Nicholas already moving in her direction with Tesla, Patrick's devoted companion and defender, trotting just ahead of them, his shaggy black fur and white nose and chest still damp and matted with sand from a romp in the surf.

Several small clusters of people occupied the area surrounding the fountain outside the arched entrance to the Los Baños pool house. Four men in morning coats and bowler hats sat talking and smoking on a pair of benches situated so as to take advantage of the views beyond the Plaza: the Pleasure Pier extending out over the waves to their left, the Channel Islands off-shore in the distance, and Castle Rock a quarter-mile beyond the Pleasure Pier - though all were nearly invisible this morning, being shrouded in fog.

Nearer the fountain itself, a father and mother stood beside their young wheelchair-bound son as they watched his two younger siblings chase each other around in the open space with much squealing and laughter. Half a dozen women, exhibiting the rather heavy-handed air of temperance, strode purposefully around the perimeter of the entire plaza, arms raised and swinging in such a way that their intention to extract the most physical benefit from the surrounding ether was apparent.

As Leontine advanced, she saw Nicholas pause and say something to Patrick who nodded solemnly and sank onto the concrete bench that formed the perimeter of the fountain. She could see, even from this distance, that Patrick's short trousers, socks and shoes were soaking wet. He was wearing a flannel shirt and suspenders, but no vest or jacket, and she worried that he was cold. At least the wool flat cap that seemed permanently attached to his head would keep some of the chill at bay.

Nicholas' trousers were likewise drenched, sand caught and spilling from the upturned cuffs of his pants. He had removed his hat and sack coat and rolled up the sleeves of his shirt, though it had not prevented them from getting wet as well. Tesla turned one quick, longing look in Leontine's direction and wagged his tail for her for just a moment before he sat on the ground next to Patrick and rested his nose on the boy's knee.

The doctor intercepted Leontine as she entered the open Plaza area. "I apologize if I alarmed you," he said in greeting. "Thank you for coming so quickly."

"Is everyone all right?"

"No - a man drowned. Tesla found him half-submerged in the tide with his clothing caught on the rocks. Patrick was checking some markers he set up on the beach for some experiment. He said he didn't really look at the body before he ran for help. I hope that's true. The sea creatures..." He left the description of the remains unspoken.

Leontine pursed her lips and looked over at her young friend. He was so stoic for an eleven-year-old, it was sometimes impossible to gauge his mood. She glanced back at Nicholas who nodded in his son's direction, understanding that Leontine was anxious to be by his side. As soon as they moved toward the boy, Tesla jumped to his feet and ran to the task of rounding up the adults to ensure they found their way. Leontine's look warned the eager dog to temper his greeting, and he obligingly settled for circling her feet and sniffing at her shoes, leaving the job of communicating his excitement solely to his tail.

Leontine slid onto the bench beside her young friend and rested her hand on his thigh as his father stood close at his other side. Patrick pushed his eyeglasses up on his nose and turned his face to Leontine. She looked into his blue eyes as deeply as she could. He let her do it, holding her gaze for a long moment as if to reassure her that he was fine. Was he fine? She imagined nearly any other child would be terrified and no doubt in tears.

"Are you ready to go?" Leontine asked. Patrick stood and wiped his nose with the back of his hand and she let that one go by without comment.

"I need to get back," Nicholas said to Leontine. "I'll find you later." He gave his son a hug. Patrick tolerated the affection, as usual, but as

Nicholas straightened the boy flung his arms around his dad's waist, clinging tightly for just one brief moment. Leontine and Nicholas shared a lightning-fast glance, communicating that each had seen and registered the few seconds of vulnerability.

"Can we go by the adobe?" Patrick asked Leontine.

"Of course," Leontine said. "Let's walk."

Patrick watched his father trudge across several feet of soft sand, heading for the hard-packed pathway that swept along the beachfront to the west and wrapped around between the cliffs behind the Plaza and the back of Castle Rock. The local citizenry maintained and repaired the pathway on a volunteer basis year-round, a task that could at times be monumental - after a storm or even an exceedingly high tide.

The local undertaker, Charles McDermott, along with one of his employees, had managed to maneuver the horse-drawn hearse wagon into position near the unfortunate spot in order to collect the body. It had taken all three men, including Dr. Denman, to hold the skittish horse in place, extract the gruesome cargo from the water and then load it into the wagon for transport to McDermott's mortuary for autopsy.

Patrick and Leontine headed for Castillo Street, Tesla leading the way. They passed by the power house, trolley car barn, and the athletic field, devoid of players at the moment as members of the local baseball teams no doubt labored in their work-a-day worlds. The weekend would see the wooden bleachers packed with families and friends, cheering the players toward victory.

As the two approached Yanonali Street, they paused at the sound of an approaching automobile. A most impressive vehicle, that Patrick identified as a White Company Model G touring car, honked its horn as it went by. No doubt the smiling and obviously well-heeled occupants were guests at the Potter Hotel.

One could still easily count the number of steam and gasoline powered automobiles in Santa Barbara in this year of 1909, but that number was increasing at a rapid rate. Though the townspeople were resigned to the idea of expanding the paving of downtown streets in deference to the vehicles, a resolution to be taken up by the city council was facing plenty of resistance from citizens who criticized the deafening sound of horse hooves on asphalt and the alarming trend of automobiles dashing about at speeds that sometimes exceeded 20 miles per hour. Nevertheless, the council was expected to officially give their approval for a paving process already planned that would extend two blocks on either side of State Street all the way to Fourth Street, and also include Salinas Street on the eastern edge of town and San Andres Street on the west.

One of the things both Leontine and Patrick appreciated most about the other, however unacknowledged, was the lack of compulsion to fill every silence with chatter. They were approaching Montecito Street when Patrick finally spoke. He said, "I told my dad I didn't look at it."

"Did you?"

"His head was behind the rock."

"I'm relieved."

Patrick stopped walking and looked at his scuffed leather shoes. He nervously adjusted his cap and pushed his glasses up on his nose, keeping his eyes averted. Leontine paused as well. She rested her hand lightly on his shoulder and waited.

"I saw his hands," Patrick finally admitted.

Leontine saw his lips tighten, and he shook his head as if to dislodge the image from his mind. He sighed deeply, then resumed walking, but still did not look up at his friend. Leontine kept their pace slow.

"You know you don't have to protect your father."

"I know," Patrick said, followed by another big sigh.

"You're afraid if you're not strong you might lose your freedom."

Patrick stopped walking again and gaped up at Leontine. He had been unable to name the troubling weight in his chest and would never have been able to state it so plainly. But that was it, exactly. The liberation of being understood was profound. It straightened his spine and drove away a bit of the horror from the vision of the dead man's hands. He said, "I just don't like it when people worry about me."

Leontine understood precisely, though she did not agree out loud. It was astonishing to her that the hearts of an eleven-year-old boy and a twenty-one-year-old woman could be so very similar. And she knew that what one of those hearts needed now was the comfort found in the mundane.

"We can stop at Victoria's. She's making a present for Daisy if you want to see it."

Patrick replied with a dispirited shrug.

Leontine and her tenant and friend, Daisy Merrie, both had birthdays at the end of August. Leontine would be twenty-two on the twenty-fourth and on the thirty-first Daisy would turn twenty. The staff at the *Daily Independent*, where Daisy worked as a newspaper writer, was planning a party in their honor for Thursday, the twenty-sixth, after the normal business day was done. Though the *Independent* offices were located between companies as bland as the Red Cross Drug Company and Santa Barbara Gas & Electric, the Stafford Saloon was right across the street, some would say operating as simply an extension of the newspaper offices, and was undoubtedly where the celebration would wind up. Leontine was pretty sure that one full week ahead of the event was too early, even for her, to start worrying about how long she might be expected to linger at the celebration in order to be considered polite. If she enjoyed that consideration even now.

The two turned left at Montecito Street and made their way to the small Ramirez farm in the 300 block of Rancheria Street, where Leontine's seamstress and long-time friend, Victoria, worked and lived with her eldest son, daughter-in-law and their five children. The old adobe house at the front of the property was showing signs of age, decades of wind and rain having rounded edges and washed away bits of the mud mortar that held together adobe bricks made of clay, sand and straw. The process of repairing and re-applying sections of a protective plaster whitewash was underway at the front of the dwelling.

A sliver of a yard between the house and the fence along Rancheria Street was free of landscaping and nearly overrun by an endlessly budding and spreading nopal cactus. Leontine and Patrick let themselves in the front gate and walked around to the back of the property which covered more than two acres.

The area just behind the house was dominated by a large and rambling chicken coop. More than fifty chickens slept there and contributed a healthy share of the annual income for the farm with the eggs they produced, many of which sold at the Birabent Market. The chickens spent their daylight hours in pursuit of bits of grain, random bugs and kitchen scraps, scratching in the dirt and flirting with the half-dozen roosters, housed separately, that would be turned out into their midst every couple of days to ensure their population was maintained.

A barn, goat pens, tack room and machine shed lined the north side of the parcel, while the opposing property line was defined by a long, narrow duck pond shared with the adjoining farm to the south. The family horses stood around chewing in a small corral at the back of the property along with Gruñon, an aging and portly burro, and their two work mules, Bebé and Bombón.

Nearly twenty years earlier Victoria's husband, Justo, was helping a friend set up an enormous threshing machine. The thing collapsed while he was underneath it, leaving his legs paralyzed. For two years Justo Ramirez dedicated the time necessary to educate his three young sons in the running of the family and the farm. When the boys appeared to have matters in hand, Justo took his own life - or so it was surmised. His wheelchair somehow rolled into the duck pond and then capsized and he drowned in the shallow water.

Their eldest son, Justito, ran the farm now, and he helped out his cousin Diego at the Tally Ho Stables, just across the street from the Birabent Market, maintaining and sometimes driving the carriages for extra money. When his own expanding family finally overran the interior space of the main residence, Justito constructed a cozy and comfortable sewing studio attached to the back of the dwelling for his mother, which included a small sleeping room.

His two younger brothers had eventually married and set up homes of their own nearer the center of town. Margarita, the youngest, had been a year ahead of Leontine at Santa Barbara High School. Bright and ambitious, Margarita had no interest in sewing, farming or anything else in the small town of Santa Barbara. She moved to Los Angeles immediately upon graduating from high school and Victoria kept Leontine up-to-date on her daughter's developing career, first as a file clerk and then office assistant at a law firm in Pasadena.

As soon as Leontine and Patrick entered the back yard, Tesla took off to get the chickens rounded up, bark at the goats and drench himself anew in the duck pond – all duties accomplished inside of two minutes, though the circuit would have to be repeated many times. Leontine half-expected to find her friend Victoria out on the wide recessed porch where she would often complete hand-stitching or embroidery seated at a tiled table. There she could more easily see the detail work in the daylight, and her grandchildren chasing around and playing in the yard in the bargain.

This morning, however, it was not the case. Leontine tapped at the heavy plank door. After about a minute she and Patrick exchanged a wondering look. Leontine leaned to peer through the window. She did not see Victoria seated at her Singer sewing machine on the other side of the glass. She turned to Patrick and shrugged her shoulders, ready to give it up and proceed on to the old adobe on Bath Street that Patrick had commandeered two years earlier for use as his laboratory, personal library and fort.

Just as they started to walk away, the sound of a baby's cry erupted from inside the studio, causing them to pause in their tracks. They turned back around and Leontine tapped on the door once more. In another moment Victoria appeared at last. At fifty-nine her luscious mane of upswept hair was streaked with gray, but she projected the vigor of a much younger woman, her eyes bright and her face relatively free of wrinkles. She was thick at the waist with ample hips and meaty arms, the better for family and friends to sink into the warm comfort of her ferocious embrace. Women who had the good fortune to avail themselves of Victoria's services as a seamstress were lavished with praise and petted like poodles until it became impossible for them to seek any other provider when expanding their personal wardrobes.

In the many years Leontine had known Victoria she could not remember a time when the affectionate and effusive woman seemed ill at ease – until this moment. Victoria did not fully open the door and there was a furrow in her brow that looked singularly out of place on her normally beaming face.

"Victoria?" Leontine said, half a dozen questions contained in the gentle question mark implied when she spoke the name. And then the baby cried again and another woman spoke in Spanish from inside the room.

"*Está bien. Déjalos entrar.*"

Victoria glanced over her shoulder, then more fully opened the door. She kissed Leontine on the cheek as she ushered her inside, then turned her attention to Patrick.

"*Patricio! Ay, mijo!* You grow so big!" she said scooping the boy into her arms, immediately seeming much more herself. Patrick ducked his head and blushed, then gave in to the overt affection. He hugged Victoria tight for a moment, then removed one arm to push his glasses up on his nose. Victoria measured his height on her own body, over-the-moon amazed that the top of his head had reached her chin. He couldn't help but grin as she pushed him along into the house.

The rectangular area of Victoria's sewing studio was comfortable, cozy and functional. Her Singer treadle sewing machine was situated in front of a large recessed window overlooking the back yard to take advantage of the natural light. The painted surface of the foot plate where Victoria's feet rested was worn to bare metal and the wooden base cabinet had been scratched with scissors and poked with needles so many times it looked as though it had been through a war. Tiny drawers held tools for measuring, marking, cutting and sewing. A wood frame with a hundred pegs that supported wooden spools of thread in dozens of colors hung on the wall above stacks of bolts of fabric of every conceivable color and texture. The sewing machine was flanked by several "body forms" Justito had made for her, that could wear the garments as she worked on them. There was a bust form for bodice work sitting on a wide sewing table where Patrick could not seem to stop his eyes from returning, a hip form for skirts that could vary in height by switching out risers and two torsos of framed wood covered with canvas sacks that could be stuffed with cotton batting to precisely the size required, then molded into shape with shoulder forms also made of wood. And corsets, of course.

The opposite end of the room was dominated by a home altar. A large crucifix hung in the center of the wall, surrounded by images of Jesus, his Blessed Mother and several of the saints. Small end tables held candles and fresh flowers, photographs of Victoria's children and grandchildren and other items representing people she loved and for whom she would pray while kneeling on a cushion on the floor before the altar. One small frame contained Leontine's first attempt at embroidery, a hummingbird poised in front of a flower, that in truth looked amazingly polished for the work of a child. A small settee, footstool and reading lamp were arranged under the recessed window on the other side of the door from the sewing machine, again to take advantage of natural light for reading.

Facing the door was the open alcove of the sleeping room, its back wall shared with the dining area of the main house. It was a tight space, filled completely by a small chest of drawers and a cushy bed covered with a velvety, multi-colored patchwork quilt and nearly a dozen pillows of varying size and thickness, and covered with delicious fabric. On this bed lay the squalling baby mid-way through a diaper change being executed by Victoria's daughter. She appeared somewhat haggard as she glanced up from her task to greet Leontine.

"Margarita!" Leontine said in surprise.

"It's Margaret now," the other woman said around the diaper pin held between her teeth. She focused for a final few seconds so she could complete the diapering job, then lifted the baby to her shoulder and stood up from the bed. Leontine shot a glance at Victoria, seeing that the line of her mouth reflected the anticipated disapproval of her daughter's use of the Americanized name.

Patrick could easily tell that the camaraderie in the room was off, but had no interest at all in understanding why. He motioned to Victoria, who bent her ear to hear his whispered request to visit the goat pens, and made his escape to join Tesla outside.

Leontine was at a loss where to begin. Surely this child could not be Margarita's own. She would undoubtedly have received detailed descriptions of any wedding, pregnancy and subsequent birth, as she had in the case of each of Victoria's other grandchildren. Tension between mother and daughter was apparent, and Leontine was uncertain whether the best course of action was to insert herself into the situation in the hope of easing their communication, or to join Patrick outside and flee. The depth of her affection for Victoria pointed to the first choice, however, and so, once resolved, she dove in.

"I'm surprised to see you," she said to Margarita – now Margaret. "And with a baby! Who could this little one be?"

A look passed between mother and daughter. Victoria lifted her chin and folded her arms across her chest, defiant. The meaning was clear: if there was any lying to be done, her daughter was on her own. The baby began to fuss and Margarita jostled it on her shoulder as she considered what to say.

Leontine bought her a little more time saying, "Is it a boy or a girl?"

"A boy. Frankie. Francis S. Fordyce, III." She sat on the bed again, still jiggling the fussy infant. An awkward silence extended into the space between the three women. Frankie squirmed and twisted his head around, whimpering. Even for the uninitiated, his desire for food was obvious. Margarita shifted the boy in her arms. Leontine could not help wondering how young Mr. Fordyce was to be fed in the absence of his mother and no baby bottle apparatus in sight.

"I'm his father's assistant and secretary. He has business in town and rented the Leadbetter house so his family could be with him," Margarita said.

Victoria turned her back on the conversation and began to move things around on her sewing table. Evidently, that was a lie.

"The Leadbetter house. How grand," Leontine said. Another awkward silence filled the room.

"Well, I see you want time to catch up. We were just walking back from the Plaza."

The women did not attempt to change Leontine's mind and she felt positively swept out the door. When she stepped outside the studio, she raised her eyes to the large mesa that blocked the view to the ocean. She could just see the top of the Leadbetter mansion, so near, yet so far removed in many ways. She went to retrieve Patrick from the goat pens, wondering as she waded through the chickens what on earth was going on in the Ramirez family.

"Is Victoria mad at somebody?" Patrick asked, once Leontine had joined him at the rail fence.

"I don't know – it seemed like it."

Patrick pursed his lips and whistled for Tesla to tear himself away from the duck pond and the three continued on their way to Patrick's adobe.

CHAPTER 2

John Tade bent to pick up the note slipped under his door by the Neal Hotel staff. Stupid with exhaustion, he read the brief missive ten times in ten seconds, then stood, his arm poised as if to read it yet again, and stared sightlessly through his second-floor window. Next door a massive locomotive rumbled on the tracks of the Southern Pacific Railroad, rattling his window. The sound of the train's whistle broke his reverie, and Tade crushed the note in his fist. It was easy enough to remember, saying only:

Get back out here.

It was June of 1903 when good luck, or perhaps divine providence, piqued John Tade's interest in an announcement printed in the *Los Angeles Herald*. He read that the Automobile Club of Southern California was to meet at the Westminster Hotel to elect regular officers and its board of governors for the following year. The notice informed that the club was reorganizing and that, thenceforward, all members would be required to possess a car of their own. Quite suddenly, he was overcome with a desire to purchase one, though the thought had never occurred to him before.

In existence since 1900, the first three years of memberships in the Automobile Club consisted primarily of agents and salesmen, wheeling and dealing in what they thought was a passing fad of the average gentleman of leisure. The association mainly concerned itself with promoting the motor car in general, and officiating at parades, races and shows. By 1903, however, more than six hundred vehicles traveled where they could around the county of Los Angeles, with an equal number already on order for delivery as quickly as they could be turned out of the manufacturing companies back east. Furthermore, regular automobile liveries had become established throughout the county, where citizens could rent the contraptions for novelty, recreation or convenience. The success of these businesses provided further evidence that the automobile was gaining traction for more general use, and was increasingly recognized as the preferred means of transportation for personal and commercial use alike. It was becoming clear that governing rules and conventions were going to have to come from someplace, and the Automobile Club of Southern California was voting itself the logical choice.

Far from a man of means, Tade worked in the accounts department of the Southern Pacific Railroad corporate office in Los Angeles. At twenty-nine, he had yet to accumulate what he felt was a sufficient store of money to take on a wife and start a family, and so continued to live under his parents' roof in Whittier, socking away funds toward that end. John was not a tall man, tending toward portliness and with a rapidly receding hairline that only served to accentuate the roundness of his face. He wore an earnest expression, and most often tried hard to please, but, much like the over-sized toddler he appeared, frustration or uncertainty could often lead to explosive fits of temper. His aging parents worried that something was lacking in their only child. or worse, that they had erred in some crucial way in his upbringing, leaving him unable or unwilling to find his way through the normal progressions of life. They offered continual optimism and support, asking nothing in return, and hoping against hope that one day he would achieve his inner milestone at last, take a bride, and get to the business of peopling another generation of Tades. Though his announcement of the intention to purchase an automobile seemed off-track to Mr. and Mrs. Tade, they expressed encouragement, as much from sheer habit as anything else.

John settled on "The Boss of the Road", a Ford Model A two-seater Runabout model with headlamps and horn, paid his $850, then waited nearly six months for delivery. Fortunately, his bill of sale proved sufficient to gain access to Automobile Club meetings, and from then on, he never missed even one.

It was in June of the following year that the purpose of these seemingly impulsive actions was revealed to him. He experienced what could only be called a 'vision' on his way to a club meeting in Santa Monica, attended at the end of a stressful day of work. Tade had been tasked with producing a cost projection analysis for the upcoming calendar year 1905, of how much the Southern Pacific Railroad would spend paving trolley lines in southern California. Though towns and municipalities bore the financial burden for street paving within their own boundaries, and states were stepping up to pave distances between them, railroads and trolley lines were required to absorb the cost of paving between rails and for a distance of two feet on either side of the tracks. There were close to a dozen individual power and electric companies in the southern California region responsible for various trolley lines, but Southern Pacific was so heavily invested in all of them that the massive company devoted several account specialists solely to those interests.

Street paving was an industry gone wild across the entire continent, and the calculations were proving nearly impossible to pin down. Naturally-occurring asphalt was no longer the only option for material, with patent applications for new versions of manufactured asphalt springing up almost daily. The installation process for the various paving systems differed widely as well, creating countless variables to be considered.

Mulling over the complex task as he drove himself to Santa Monica, Tade was forced to wait at a crossroad near the Pacific Line. An imposing Pierce-Arrow Model 36 situated between himself and a trolley car stopped on the tracks behind it fell into his line of sight, creating the illusion that the overhead system of wires was connected to the top of the car. He smiled inwardly, amused. Then he thought about it for a minute. If you had a cab big enough for several passengers, a strong enough undercarriage and the right number of wheels, could you forego the rails entirely? The passenger car could still tie in to the overhead system of wires for power, but roll along the same roads as everyone else, no rails – or paving – required. A trackless trolley. The company could save hundreds of thousands of dollars. The idea seemed so complete and obvious, he assumed at the time it must have already been rejected for some reason.

Early on, Tade learned he would first have to convince a man named Robert Lovell, Esq. of the feasibility of the idea. Lovell, a mustachioed man of impeccable grooming, precise posture and controlled movement, was general counsel for both Southern Pacific and Union Pacific Rail Roads, and was widely thought of as "heir apparent" to Edward "Ned" Harriman's corporate empire. The railroad magnate relied heavily on his general counsel – an arrangement meticulously nurtured by Lovell – and consulted with him on most matters, large and small.

At the end of an impassioned presentation, Lovell informed that it would be he himself, not Tade, who would ultimately present the idea to his boss - if it was deemed worthy. Ultimately, however, the lawyer dismissed the concept, declaring the overhead power system ugly and cumbersome to maintain. He refused to bring it to the attention of Harriman or anyone on the board of directors. In the ensuing months, Tade watched with increasing alarm as the idea occurred to others around the globe, fearful that someone else would end up taking credit for what he could only think of as his idea.

It was at an Automobile Club meeting that Tade finally found a way to maneuver around Lovell. He had engaged in conversation with one Francis Fordyce, Esq., a contract attorney and board member for the railroad, who became immediately enthralled with the concept of the trackless trolley. When it came to light that Fordyce was well acquainted with Harriman, and had worked in the railroad's interest on many occasions, Tade was deeply encouraged.

Fordyce became all the more captivated upon hearing of Lovell's stonewalling activities. He recognized the trackless trolley idea as something that would hold great interest for Ned Harriman, and further, hoped he had finally found the tool he had been searching for to pry Harriman apart from his right-hand man. Fordyce knew he had caught the eye of Harriman and wished to do all he could to foster increasing attention. To date, Lovell had somehow always managed to insert himself, keeping Fordyce at arms' length. But in this case, Lovell's opposition to the idea was already professed, so he could hardly say otherwise now.

Almost an entire year passed before Fordyce could engineer an opportunity for Tade to present his idea directly to Harriman. It took another year to produce a business model worthy of financial commitment, and yet another to fully develop the prototype concept that would be installed for testing in Hope Ranch, one of the railroad's real estate holdings located just over one hundred miles north of Los Angeles. By then, Fordyce enjoyed access to Harriman at a level nearly equal to that of his rival.

Lovell had invested a decade of self-sacrifice and subjugation in order to make himself indispensable to his boss, however, and would be damned if he'd let his years-long endeavor come to naught. He could sense their bond weakening despite continual efforts to insinuate himself into Harriman's presence, as Fordyce exploited the great man's enthusiasm for the insipid trackless trolley. In an effort to stop the erosion of the confidence he had so long enjoyed, Lovell finally pretended to see the light, and turned his efforts toward achieving the success of the trackless trolley, though he remained watchful for any opportunity to place Fordyce, Tade or the system itself in a bad light.

And now, at last, more than five years since the first inkling, the Trackless Trolley awaited only a final green light from Harriman to become reality. He was scheduled to evaluate the prototype on the twenty-eighth of August - one week from today.

Francis Fordyce was charged with negotiating and drafting contractual agreements for sub-contractors and suppliers for, not only the prototype, but also its expansion into all of southern California, should efforts in Hope Ranch prove successful - as was anticipated. To his utter annoyance, all final drafts had to be signed off by Lovell as well. John Tade was in charge of distributing funds, but again, it was Lovell who signed the actual checks.

They had engaged the Santa Barbara Paving Company early on and found the owner, James Patillo, so knowledgeable that they secured him to oversee all of the construction. The project was going well and Tade had not actually planned to go out to the site today. Especially after all that had occurred the night before. He looked at the note crumpled in his fist, swore under his breath, then grabbed his hat and left the room.

When Tade reached the bottom of the staircase and entered the Neal Hotel lobby, he became immediately aware of a general atmosphere of calamity. Clusters of people spoke in hushed tones, casting furtive glances about in every direction. He passed in front of the long admittance desk and loitered in front of a display of information brochures, eavesdropping to the best of his ability to see if he could figure out what was going on. Unable to make sense of the conversation fragments, he finally approached a dapper young man stationed behind the admittance desk and simply asked what was happening.

"Someone found a dead body at Castle Rock," the clerk said. "McDermott's wagon just went by."

John Tade knew he looked horrified, and he hoped like hell he also looked surprised.

CHAPTER 3

Patrick's adobe was situated on the east side of Bath Street between Cota and Haley Streets. He had discovered the place, walking with his father one morning two years earlier, when he was only nine. The place was obviously abandoned, a chaotic layer of dandelions, fox tails, wild bougainvillea and nopal cactus obscuring a more disciplined landscape that had been imposed at some time in the past. Young Patrick became attached to the crumbling dwelling immediately, and before long Nicholas Denman learned from a neighbor that his son had been carrying furniture and personal belongings inside.

When Patrick was three the Denman men lost their wife and mother when she died giving birth to a stillborn daughter. Though Patrick tried as hard as he could to remember her, he couldn't really. His dad tried to help him remember too, and the stories and memories he shared about his wife actually did create a presence of sorts in Patrick's mind that sometimes seemed almost like having a mom. The father, sensing Patrick's strong attraction to the old adobe, believed that at least part of its appeal could be found in the imagined permanence of real estate. The house was obviously not going anywhere, despite its frayed condition. Fortunately, the good doctor was able to buy the damaged adobe and unkempt yard at a reasonable price, but he kept his ownership a secret so that Patrick could claim it as his own. In return, Patrick kept the secret that he knew about the purchase all along.

The two-room dwelling was nestled under a spreading oak tree that had completely covered a hole burned in the roof of what was once the kitchen. Patrick had enjoyed the tree-house-like sensation that the hole beneath the branches provided until his preceding birthday on the twenty-sixth of November, when his father presented him with a

Kodak No. 3A Autographic camera. The interior side of the hole was subsequently covered over and a wall built to section off a small space surrounding the kitchen sink and counter, so that the newly created space could serve as Patrick's dark room. An exceedingly long rubber hose ran from the sink, through a small hole at the base of the wall, and connected to a faucet belonging to the neighbor next door, which provided running water for the photo-finishing process.

Situated beneath two large recessed windows facing the dark room was his long plank work-table, piled to oblivion with dozens of projects in varying stages of completion. They were so numerous that they filled, not only the table, but the entire perimeter of the room as well. Spear making, electrical wiring, furniture repair, fishing lures and paper maché. Instruction pamphlets, reference books, notebooks and a typewriter. Paints, plants, wire cages, door knobs and mirrors. A gramophone, a clarinet, a Spanish guitar and an autoharp. Glue, nails, a vice, steel wool and part of a spinning wheel – and so much more. The artifacts appeared chaotic to the untrained eye, but the items were actually quite carefully arranged as it was the only way everything could possibly fit.

The second room was decorated with used furniture Patrick had scrounged up over time. There was an overstuffed chair and miss-matched ottoman resting on an oval hooked rug and positioned cozily in front of a low brick hearth and shallow fireplace. Along the north wall stood two sturdy bookshelves, given to Patrick by Miss Della Chambers, Assistant Librarian, when new shelving was purchased for the library on Carrillo Street. These shelves had been occupying Patrick and Leontine for the past couple of hours.

For Patrick's same eleventh birthday, Leontine had purchased a collection of *Popular Science* magazines dating back to 1900, and every issue of *Popular Mechanics* published since its inception in 1902. The elderly widow who sold the collection had been pleased that an eager young boy would enjoy the volumes so devotedly collected by her late husband. Patrick and Leontine quietly sorted the magazines and placed them on the new shelves in ascending date order as Tesla napped in the chair. Leontine noticed that Patrick would often pause, his gaze turned inward for several moments, until he resumed his task half-heartedly. He was even less talkative than usual.

"Your father said you had markers on the beach. Do you have an experiment going?" she asked.

"It was dumb. I don't even know why I was doing it."

"What was it?" Leontine prodded. Patrick sighed, as if too weary to explain it all. He carried a stack of magazines to where she knelt at the bookshelves and set them beside her.

"Can I help you with it?"

"I'm not going to do it."

Leontine pursed her lips. She didn't want to force him to talk if he didn't want to, but worried that if he tried to ignore whatever was troubling him, he might suffer for it later. She considered what to say. Should she press him to talk? Was a gentle approach best, with sympathy and affection, or was it better to remain matter-of-fact and treat death as the grim, though inevitable, event that it was? She didn't know.

By noon, the sun had finally burned its way through the fog bank. It was getting quite warm when hunger finally interrupted their progress. Leontine had a piano lesson to teach at two o'clock, so they decided to head for the Birabent Market to see if Uncle Remy had eaten anything yet. If there was still no word from Dr. Denman when their lunch was finished, Patrick could easily occupy himself at the store while she taught her lesson. He enjoyed combing through the shelves to arrange the goods in impeccable order – all labels facing outward and perfectly aligned with the shelf edge.

When they arrived, Uncle Remy was dousing the vegetable bins with water again to keep the produce crisp and sparkling. A look he shared with Leontine made it plain that he was aware of the incident at Castle Rock and Patrick's part in the discovery of the dead man. Unlike Leontine, Remy did not overthink his approach with Patrick, and he spoke matter-of-factly.

"What a day. You hungry?"

"I guess."

"Take this," Remy said. He handed Patrick the business end of the rubber hose that stretched from the produce sink behind the market, then headed for the prep area in the back of the store.

Leontine saw something that looked like relief wash over Patrick's expression, and believed that it sprung from a desire to be able to act as if nothing was wrong, at least for the moment. She didn't know if it was intentional, but dear Uncle Remy had somehow made them both feel better.

Leontine popped behind the counter to have a quick look at the register as Patrick wetted the produce. No sooner had he disconnected the hose and coiled it into its circular storage pattern, than Daisy strode into the store and made right for him. He offered no resistance when she pulled him in for a hug.

"Patrick! Are you all right? I thought I had the story of the day, but you passed it. Everyone at the paper is talking about how brave you are."

"About me?" Patrick stood away from Daisy and pushed his glasses up on his nose. "Why am I brave?"

"Because you are!" Daisy said, "You ran all the way to the Plaza and got help."

"Oh."

He knew he could have told them that he had not been brave at all. Even Uncle Remy. Even his dad. He was sure they all wanted to know how he had been checking the wooden markers he had hammered deep into the sand to measure the depth of the overnight tide, and how Tesla had barked and whined and circled in a strange way, and then practically dragged him over to Castle Rock.

At first, he didn't see anything. Then it was just formless color, wavering in the shallow surf. Was it a blanket? Someone's laundry? He was nearly upon it when he saw the dead man's hands. Thankfully, the face was obscured by an outcropping of the rock. He wasn't sure if he screamed, but he was pretty sure he did. He had a sound in his ears like the after-shock of a scream. He jumped behind the huge rock so he couldn't see the body. He had to tell someone. He looked up the beach to the Plaza del Mar, a quarter of a mile ahead. He could run the distance easily, but he would have to go by the dead man. He could take the path on the other side of the rock and not even be able to see it, but somehow, he couldn't make himself do it. It was as if an invisible line was drawn across the sand between the body and the cliff face, and he didn't think he could go past it.

Tesla was prancing back and forth in the surf between Patrick and the body, whining. Patrick knew it couldn't reach out and grab him. What was the matter with him? He leaned against the rock, breathing hard and feeling like he had been running too long. He didn't know what was wrong. He couldn't think straight, and he started to cry. It seemed like a long time until he could finally talk himself into running for help. He held his breath and closed his eyes and tore out as fast as he could go, and he didn't stop crying until he was almost to the Plaza. No…he had not been brave. He knew he could tell them. He just didn't want to. He changed the subject by questioning Daisy.

"What was your story?"

Daisy directed her response more to Leontine. "The council passed an ordinance that drinking establishments are to stop serving liquor to women starting in October. Can you believe it?"

Leontine felt her brow furrow. "What do they hope to accomplish in that?" she asked.

"They used the word "decorum" a lot, but I don't think it's the women that are lousing it up. I'm going back to the paper to write it up, and O'Brien better print it when I'm done," Daisy warned.

Patrick asked, "Do the people at the paper know anything? I mean, do they know who that man was?"

"He's from out of town, renting the Leadbetter mansion. I don't know his name," Daisy said.

Leontine gasped, causing Daisy and Patrick to look over at her in alarm.

"It's Fordyce," she said.

CHAPTER 4

Caroline Fordyce stared at an oversized painting of a fox-hunting scene hanging above the stone fireplace in the library of the stately Leadbetter mansion. Her eye was drawn to the pitiable fox near the bottom of the picture, cornered and snarling in desperation as he faced his tormentors and certain death. Horrible.

Francis Fordyce had rented the furnished estate, set near the crest of the hill to the west of the Potter Hotel, so that his young wife of two years and the new child could be with him while he drafted agreements and drew up legal documents between some of the most powerful companies in California; a job that might take months to complete.

It was early afternoon, hours since Dr. Nicholas Denman and the local sheriff, Nat Stewart, had first appeared at the broad door of the magnificent home. Hats in hand, speaking softly with carefully chosen words, they explained about the discovery of a drowned man on the beach below the cliffs not far from where they stood. Inquiries at Plaza del Mar and the Potter Hotel had provided enough information for them to believe that the victim might be Francis Fordyce. Upon now learning that Mr. Fordyce was not at home, the worst seemed all the more probable. The body had yet to be officially identified, and they did not ask it of Caroline now. Others were trying to find anyone else that might be able to accomplish the undesirable task. The sheriff asked if she wanted to be present at the McDermott Undertaking Company when they examined the body, but no, she did not.

Caroline had withdrawn, her own thoughts somehow louder in her mind than the voices and actions surrounding her. She found it difficult to speak through the distracting noise in her head, almost as if she was under water herself, and she saw concern in the eyes of the doctor as he studied her. He offered a sedative, which she declined, and then the men vowed diligence in getting to the bottom of whatever might have happened to her husband – if in fact it was her husband. They promised to return as soon as the identity was confirmed and explained there would be questions if she was up to it, and, of course, many decisions to be made. It was a relief when they finally left so she could think without the commotion of talking and movement around her.

She had awakened alone in the small hours of the morning and sat upright in her bed for hours, anxiety mounting, her hand resting on the empty space beside her until daybreak when she finally rose and walked barefoot into the bathroom. She splashed her face with cold water, then for several moments peered steadily into the reflection of the ice-blue of her own eyes in the mirror above the sink. She applied rouge to her cheekbones and lips, then freshened her lush pile of sable curls. She selected a length of deep purple ribbon to secure them in place and pulled several strands underneath the ribbon to frame her pretty face, then slid into her rose-pink satin dressing gown and slippers, and proceeded downstairs.

As early as it was, the housemaid had been up before her and already kindled fires in the master suite, dining hall and here, in the library. Since then Caroline had not left the room, finding the shelves of leather-bound volumes, plush Persian rugs and thickly padded furnishings somehow comforting. An enormous ebony desk dominated the space, crafted with intricately carved renderings of ancient warriors and serpentine dragons. A chaise lounge and matching velvet-covered chairs pointed away from the room toward the windows, rather than facing one another in order to promote conversation, as was customary.

Caroline shivered, despite the warm fire, as she stared through the tall windows out toward the sea, shrouded now beneath a dense layer of marine fog. She removed a soft woolen throw from the arm of one of the velvet chairs and wrapped it around her shoulders as she stood at the window wrestling with her thoughts.

She wondered how Francis' body had ended up at Castle Rock - and what she would say to these men when they returned with their inescapable questions. As much as she detested the idea, she needed to talk to Margaret before anything was divulged, and she wondered where the girl was now with that damnable baby. She also needed some time with Francis' personal effects and papers, before the inevitable onslaught of lawyers and accountants swept in to lock them away, outside of her control. She wished she could ask Francis what she should do, and for a moment felt as though she might cry. But just now she had to be very smart or this world of wealth and privilege might evaporate as quickly as it had materialized.

Caroline turned back to the room, moved to the desk and slid into the high-backed leather chair. She sat up straight and pulled the wool blanket more tightly around her shoulders, envisioning herself as the fox, squared-off against overwhelming assault and determined to prevail.

And then, almost before she knew it, the sheriff and the very-kind doctor reappeared to impart their news. How long had she been sitting and staring at the painting? She was still in her dressing gown and satin slippers. This would not do.

Caroline stood and motioned Dr. Denman and Sheriff Stewart toward chairs, though both men chose to stand. She sat once more, remaining behind the desk, as though its mass might afford some protection from the information they possessed.

"Forgive me Mrs. Fordyce," Nicholas said, "but the news is not good."

Caroline turned away from the men, dabbing at her eyes with a delicate handkerchief as if tears were collecting there. The men informed her that Milo Potter had identified the body, having dined and shared board rooms with Fordyce on many occasions. Caroline asked that they communicate her gratitude to the hotel man.

After several moments of silence Sheriff Stewart said, "Mrs. Fordyce, I need to ask you some questions. I can wait if you tell me to, but the sooner I get to it, the sooner I can find out what happened."

"Please, ask your questions."

"When was the last time you saw your husband?"

"Yesterday at the Potter Country Club event. I left ahead of him."

"He didn't come home?"

"No."

"Do you know who he was with after you left?"

"His business associates, I presume."

"Do you know their names?"

"Some of them." Caroline's gaze drifted to the window and the men shared a glance, wondering if they should proceed. Sheriff Stewart decided to press on.

"Can you think of anyone that might know who he was with?"

"Our nanny was there. She left after I did."

"Is she here now?"

"I'm not sure. She's been spending time with her family. She grew up here. Her name is Margaret Ramirez." Caroline's look shifted to the window again, so she did not see it when the doctor motioned to the lawman that the interview should be brought to an end.

Once outside the door, the men started down the broad stairs to the hitching post to retrieve their horses, but the commanding view of the oceanfront, the Potter Hotel and the Channel Islands in the distance was impossible to ignore. They paused and stood in silence for a long moment.

"I'll find you when we know cause of death," the doctor finally said.

"I thought he drowned."

"He might have, but he could have fallen from the cliff above." It remained unsaid that he could have as easily jumped or been pushed, but the thought occurred to each of them.

"I want to find that nanny before memories start fading," said the sheriff. "Do you know her?"

Nicholas shook his head. "It might be faster to wait her out here," he suggested.

As the doctor retrieved his rented horse and buggy from the circular drive near the fountain, Sheriff Stewart mounted Lois, his sorrel Quarter Horse mare, having decided to check out the cliffs above the beach at the end of the property while he waited for Miss Ramirez to return.

Once arrived at the end of the path, the sheriff dismounted and walked to the end of the point, peered over the edge and examined the area surrounding Castle Rock. If the body had gone over, it would have landed on the path behind the rock. He supposed sufficient momentum might have caused it to roll far enough to drop into the water, but he didn't know enough about the laws of physics to say if that was a real possibility.

Stewart shifted his gaze out over the Pacific. Counting fishermen and pleasure seekers there was plenty of boating activity out in the channel on any given day. The victim could have washed in if he drowned close enough to shore but he would still be at the bottom if he drowned out beyond the action of the waves. If the autopsy failed to tell the whole tale, Stewart would need to think of someone to ask about such things. He poked around in the dirt and dried brush looking for anything suspicious, but could see nothing out of the ordinary.

Before long, he saw a carriage round the curve leading up to the mansion. As he walked Lois back to the house, he observed the driver assisting his female passenger as she climbed from the carriage holding an infant. She spoke with the driver briefly, then walked around the dwelling to a rear entrance. She wore a trendy new fashion called a hobble skirt, so-called because it gathered tightly near the ankles, and it was making the going quite precarious for her. He only knew the term because of the chiding he had delivered to his youngest daughter when she purchased a similar outfit at Trenwith's not a week earlier and modeled it for his approval. She had been crestfallen when he poked fun at the ridiculous styling, but better that, he thought, than have her toppling over on the street.

Once Stewart had hitched Lois up to the post again, he was momentarily confounded. Should he knock at the front door or approach from the back where he had seen the nanny enter? It occurred to him it might be useful to get to her before she had a chance to talk to Caroline Fordyce. He hurried across the manicured lawn, squinting into the tall windows as he went, hoping to spot her if she went looking for Mrs. Fordyce in the library, but the reflections on the window glass kept him from seeing inside.

The sheriff knocked several times at the back door before Miss Ramirez finally appeared, no longer holding the baby, and perplexed that someone would approach there and not the main entrance. She spotted his badge and her look shot up to his face, eyes guarded.

"May I help you?" Margaret asked.

"Miss Ramirez," the sheriff said, removing his hat, "I need to talk to you about an unfortunate incident concerning Mr. Fordyce."

"Yes?"

"May I come in?"

Margaret stepped out onto the porch instead, and motioned toward a pair of elaborate white wicker chairs situated near the edge of the porch. The two moved in that direction but neither sat down.

"Mr. Fordyce was found on the beach this morning, drowned."

Margaret gasped and her hand covered her mouth, eyes wide in disbelief.

"His wife is informed. We left her a short time ago" the sheriff continued. "I know it's a shock but I have some questions. Do you think you can answer them now?"

Margaret lowered her hand and closed her eyes.

"May I sit down?"

"Of course."

She lowered herself onto one of the wicker chairs and the sheriff gave her a few moments to collect herself before asking his first question.

"How long have you been employed as nanny?" he began.

"I'm not a nanny." Margaret seemed insulted by the suggestion.

"I thought – " the sheriff stopped himself short, then said, "I must have misunderstood. Are you employed by the Fordyce family?"

"I'm secretary and assistant to Mr. Fordyce. Or, I was."

"Did you see your employer yesterday?"

"Yes. He played in a golf tournament at the Potter Country Club. We joined him for dinner afterward," she said.

"We."

"His wife and son and me."

"Did you speak to him after the event?"

"No. I – my brother was there and I – well… Mr. Fordyce was inside with his wife. I went home with the baby." That sounded to the sheriff more like a nanny than an assistant, but he did not belabor the point.

"You left before they did."

"Yes."

Sheriff Stewart was careful to keep his expression neutral while he registered the woman's nervousness. He said, "I'm told he's a lawyer. Do you know who he's representing?"

"It's not like that. He's a contract attorney."

"I see. What kind of contracts?"

"I couldn't say."

The sheriff could sense her clamming up and decided to change direction. "You grew up here," he said.

"Yes, but I've lived in Los Angeles for five years." Then Margaret looked over her shoulder and turned a listening ear toward the house. "Is that all?"

"Do you have his appointment book?"

"I know where he keeps it."

"I'd like to get a look at it."

Margaret appeared uneasy. She had worked in a law office long enough to know better than to just start handing things over to the police.

"You'll have to ask Caroline," she replied, then excused herself and went inside.

The sheriff headed around to the front of the mansion to retrieve his horse, thinking he was sure Mrs. Fordyce had called the other woman her nanny, and that she had been the first to leave Hope Ranch. He'd have to ask Nicholas how he remembered it.

CHAPTER 5

It took more than half an hour for John Tade to travel the four-and-one-half miles to Hope Ranch. His 1908 Ford Model T Touring Car had a top speed of 45 miles per hour – for all the good it did him. State and Mission Streets were well-used and the sturdy car made excellent time. Once he turned onto Modoc, however, the going was not so easy. Deep rutting, loose dirt and the need to cross several washes slowed his progress to a crawl, and the second half of the trek took many times as long as the first.

In 1887 the widow of Irish immigrant Thomas Hope sold more than two thousand acres of the western portion of her land to the Pacific Improvement Company for $255,000. Hope, a sheepherder and cattle man, had arrived in Santa Barbara in 1849. Initially, his two thousand sheep were pastured on the mission-owned lands north of Modoc Road known as Cieneguitas, which included what remained of a once-thriving Chumash Indian village. Hope was, in fact, appointed as an Indian Agent for the Chumash population in and around Cieneguitas at the edge of Rancho La Goleta, in a fruitless effort to protect them, at least in part, in their contractual dealings with white men.

Ultimately, Thomas Hope came to acquire the property known as Rancho de las Positas y la Calera, situated between what would become the extension of Modoc Road, the Pacific Ocean, Arroyo Burro Creek and Cieneguitas. After his death, the designation of the area as "Hope Ranch" endured, even after large pieces of the property were sold off.

The Pacific Improvement Company was organized in 1878 as a holding company for the heads of the Southern Pacific Railroad; Charles

Crocker, Collis Huntington, Leland Stanford and Mark Hopkins. The corporation set about acquiring lands surrounding the existing and projected routes of the railroad in order to develop infrastructure, foster community growth and commerce and, of course, make some serious money. Much of the San Pedro Harbor near Los Angeles was situated on Pacific Improvement Company land, as was the Hotel del Monte near Monterey. A similarly grand hotel had initially been envisioned for Hope Ranch, though it was later decided that the Potter Hotel, located in the city of Santa Barbara proper, filled the need for the area more than adequately.

Milo Potter found the Pacific Improvement Company board more than receptive to his idea of expanding out to the Hope Ranch area, and they had readily cleared the way for his recently completed Potter Country Club. Golf, polo and other equestrian pursuits and pastoral picnicking were then added to the extensive list of amusements enjoyed by patrons of the Potter Hotel. Once the decision was made to abandon the development of a hotel, the company surveyed and parceled out the rancho lands with the intention of creating a subdivision for the wealthy who would presumably provide even more improvements to the coveted acreage.

Pacific Improvement was very interested in Ned Harriman's proposal to engineer and install a working prototype for the trackless trolley system envisioned by the eager young Tade. The more so because the project was also supported by Milo Potter, who saw at once how useful a dedicated trolley line between his hotel and his country club in Hope Ranch might be. Harriman intimated that he was considering purchasing one of the sections of land on the ranch to enjoy as his primary residence as he began to contemplate retirement from the railroad business, giving credence to his assurances to all concerned that the prototype would be dismantled and the land restored to its former glory once its purpose was served.

꙳ ꙳ ꙳

Tade turned off Modoc onto Hubbard Avenue, the main road into Hope Ranch. Until just over one month ago, the area had been an open expanse of grassland dotted with oak trees. Since that time, a section of the land between the Potter Country Club and a tiny lake, known as Laguna Blanca, had been rendered unrecognizable. An enormous, twisting, machine-graded scar was etched into the pristine landscape in preparation for asphalt paving. The local Edison Company had recently extended the main power supply from town, which would soon be tied in to an electrical system installed for the trolley site.

Tade parked his car near the polo fields just south of the laguna. He climbed out of his car and looked up to see Robert Lovell standing at the edge of the Potter Country Club grounds, peering out over the work site like the lord of the realm. Tade removed his Derby hat and waved it broadly in salutation, then smashed it back into place with some annoyance when Lovell continued his lofty oversight with no acknowledgment of the greeting whatsoever.

In truth, Lovell's interest in the progression of the venture was more keen than ever before. He was aware of something these other men were not: Ned Harriman was gravely ill and apparently had been for quite some time. The railroad magnate did not even know himself the seriousness of his situation, the company doctors deciding it would be best for him to remain unaware and perhaps, therefore, optimistic. They deemed it prudent to explain the full extent of his malady to Robert Lovell, however, in an effort to reduce disruption of the vast commercial entities under Harriman's control, should the mantle of leadership pass as expected.

Assuming his enviable position as "right hand man" remained intact, it appeared that all Lovell need do was keep the trolley system from operating until Harriman's scheduled visit the following week had come and gone. A smile crept onto his face as he envisioned the stack of unsigned contracts that Francis Fordyce had worked so hard to negotiate, languishing on his desk at the Potter Hotel – where they were now destined to stay. He watched, as if waiting, absorbed in his thoughts of the power and privilege soon to come.

Down at the trolley site, James Patillo, owner of the Santa Barbara Paving Company, peeled off his work gloves and walked to meet Tade, moving to the laguna side of the job shack where their conversation was less likely to be overheard.

Patillo was as thin and wiry as Tade was pudgy and round, pushing sixty and feeling every year of it this morning. He wore long sideburns that connected to a thick mustache which created the somewhat unfortunate effect of cutting his face in two. His jaw, crammed overly full of browned teeth, worked continuously beneath the moustache to process and eliminate copious amounts of chewing tobacco. He habitually spit the tobacco juice on the ground at his feet, followed by a cursory, "sorry" to anyone in his presence at the time.

Patillo had now had most of the morning to consider the unsavory events of the evening before, and he intended to waste no time in hashing it out with Tade. He said, "Pimi didn't show up for work today."

"I'm not surprised."

"It's a bad sign."

"Why?"

"If he's that upset he might talk to someone."

Tade glanced nervously over each shoulder before he spoke, saying, "They already found the body. It washed up this morning at Castle Rock." He observed his glowering accomplice. He didn't know the man at all and hated it that they were now associated because of a random event.

"I'll go back into town and see if I can find out what people know," Tade continued. "But you better talk to that kid. We all need to tell the same story."

"What story is that?"

"We'll say he was drunk. It's probably true."

Patillo would do that, but suspected they were underestimating young Pimi. He said as much to Tade.

"You know him – just talk to him. And his mother. And the fellow that drove them home while you're at it." With that, Tade stomped back to his car, and with much door slamming and gear grinding, headed back toward Santa Barbara as he tried to think of a reason to approach local law enforcement with questions about the body found on the beach.

Patillo put his hands on his hips and watched Tade drive away. He didn't like the way things were shaping up at all. He spat tobacco juice on the ground by his feet and muttered, "Sorry," to no one.

Pimiento Morales was just fifteen. His mother worked in the kitchen at the Potter Country Club, and had secured the job for him at the trolley installation. It was Pimi who'd had the great misfortune to stumble upon the body of Francis Fordyce the previous evening.

It had been an eventful day in Hope Ranch. Aside from the ongoing trolley track work going on near the polo grounds, Milo Potter had organized an afternoon golf tournament to be followed by a banquet at the club facility. Hotel guests and the local citizenry were encouraged to participate and, because of the sheer volume of players, the game had continued well into the dinner hour.

It was nearly nine o'clock by the time Pimi's mother was finishing up in the kitchen. As the last stragglers climbed onto their horses, into carriages or aboard the Potter autobus, Pimi was straightening up around the jobsite to pass time until he would transport his mother home in their buckboard wagon. Moving about in the darkness, Pimi stumbled over something and fell heavily onto his shoulder. He picked himself up and turned in a flash of anger to give the mound of whatever it was a good hard kick, when, in the dim light of the moon, his eyes focused on the ghostly face of a dead man, eyes open and staring.

Pimi let out a shout of alarm. His first instinct was to run to the clubhouse for his mother, and he started to do just that – but it was so far away. He changed course, whimpering and muttering in Spanish, as he ran around the job shack toward a man leaning against a carriage at the bottom of the clubhouse driveway. Then he spotted his boss walking with a lantern closer at hand, and he changed direction once again. His panic and distress were apparent from any distance.

James Patillo gripped his lantern and ran toward the boy. John Tade saw the commotion as he was climbing into his car and hurried in the same direction. Justito Ramirez also ran from where he had been standing by his carriage, waiting for his fare - the luckless corpse.

Justito was the first to intercept the boy. He attempted to calm Pimi, putting his arm around him and speaking soothingly in Spanish as the other two went to investigate what had upset him so terribly. They saw the corpse immediately. It was just a few feet from the trolley car stair, laying awkwardly on one side, bottom shoulder thrust into the ground, hips twisted and legs extending straight out as if he had tried to roll over onto his stomach and died in the middle of the effort.

"Maybe he had a heart attack or something," Tade said.

Patillo knelt beside the body and gingerly rolled him over onto his

back. He lifted the man's arm, then let it drop. Whatever happened had
done so recently. There was no sign of rigor mortis. Patillo lifted the
lantern and the two peered into the man's face to see if they knew who he
was. Tade swore under his breath, then massaged his own temples
in distress.

Patillo stood and said, "I've seen him before."

"It's Fordyce. He's a lawyer. The lawyer."

"What happened to him?"

"How should I know?"

Patillo's eyes narrowed with suspicion, as did Tade's in return. The
men studied one another for a long moment, then each swept his gaze
over the looming trolley car and the surrounding landscape in search
of anything out of the ordinary. Except for a few remaining clubhouse
employees, all of Hope Ranch appeared quiet and deserted. Patillo spat
into the darkness. "Well, there goes your schedule," he said.

Justito approached them then, averting his eyes from the body. He
said, "I'm taking the boy home with his mom. Do you want me to send
the sheriff?"

Tade said, "We'll take care of it."

Justito nodded and started back toward the boy, then turned and
asked, "What should I tell his mom?"

Patillo said, "Don't tell her anything."

"Tell them both not to worry," Tade said.

Justito and Pimi headed up to the clubhouse to retrieve the mother as
the other two returned their attention to the corpse.

"Maybe they won't stop the work," Patillo said, without conviction.

"This was the guy keeping it going."

The truth was, Patillo was in no position to have the project stall. He
had other paving contracts ready to go for the city of Santa Barbara, but
he also had a problem. The money he had been paid from the city's coffers
to purchase materials for the paving extending out from State Street
was spent - but on materials for the job he was hurrying to complete in
Hope Ranch. He had used Pacific Improvement money to pay for the job
before that, and the same with the job before that, a situation going back
two years when he lost a law suit in Los Angeles County. A busted water
main undermined a road he had paved right in front of the government

buildings in Glendale. His work was not found at fault, but his insurance policy listed no exclusions for types of failure that would be covered. The city of Glendale's attorneys won the suit and, though it was Patillo's insurance company that footed the bill, lawyer fees and time away from his company had left Patillo in a financial strait jacket. He needed to finish this job.

"Looks like we either take him into town or send the sheriff out to get him," Patillo finally said.

"No."

"Why not?"

"Trust me. They have to find to him someplace else."

"They who? Where?"

"Anybody. Anyplace. As long as it isn't here."

The idea made Patillo uneasy, but so did the idea of stopping the project. He stared at the body of the dead lawyer, weighing the guilt of moving it against the legal and financial debacle of leaving it where it was. Finally, he said, "We're going to have to put him in your car. There's no room in the back of my truck."

It was no problem maneuvering the sturdy car, even around obstacles manufactured for the very purpose of thwarting driving. Tade got within twenty feet of the body, but they were still going to have to carry it through the worst of the mess. Patillo wrapped his arms around Fordyce's chest and nearly doubled over from the weight of the burden, as Tade wrestled with the lawyer's legs, swearing and complaining under his breath. They finally got Fordyce situated on the back seat of the car, only to decide it would be better to put him on the floorboard, out of sight. Neither man could bring himself to leave the body in an uncomfortable-looking position, though it made their efforts more strenuous.

"I'll have to follow you in my truck," Patillo said.

"We'll get it later."

"Where are we taking him?"

"I don't know. Get in."

The way out of Hope Ranch was bumpy and unnerving because it was too dark to see clearly what was coming up ahead. By the time they finally got to Modoc Road their teeth were on edge from the jostling. The car idled, headlamps shining into an indistinct distance.

"Where are we taking him?" Patillo asked again.

"How do I know? You tell me." The men sat in silence for several moments, each hoping the other would come up with the answer. Feeling anxious, Patillo reached into the front pocket of his canvas work pants and fished out his tin of Jolly Jacks.

Tade's lip curled in disgust as he observed the process of Patillo packing his cheek with tobacco. He shifted his gaze to the darkness outside the windshield. "Let's just hide him out here," he finally suggested.

"On the road?"

"By the road."

"It's too close," Patillo said, his jaw working the wad in his cheek.

"The foothills then. Or the creek."

Patillo shook his head.

"Well then you think of something," Tade said, exasperated, then almost immediately turned the car around and headed back the way they came.

"Where're you going?" Patillo asked, yet again.

"The ocean. He won't come up for days – if ever."

They followed the light from the headlamps toward the Pacific. If the body ever was discovered, whoever found it would no doubt assume the man fell into the water from the cliffs above and drowned.

By the time they got to their destination it was nearly eleven o'clock. All was quiet, save for the crash of the surf far below. The night air was cold, a thick bank of fog gathering in the channel just offshore. The men got out of the car and Patillo walked to peer over the edge.

"I can't see how far out the water is," he said. "We have to get closer."

Tade joined him at the cliff edge. "The tide will get him at some point anyways. Let's just get him out as far as we can."

Tade moved the car as close to the edge as he dared, then the men grappled with the stiffening body. This time Patillo grabbed the lawyer's legs and left Tade with the heavier end. With much effort and straining they carried the lawyer to the edge of the cliff. Swinging the body between them, they counted to three and heaved the corpse as hard as they could over the edge. Unfortunately, the men had failed to notice the gradual sloping of the cliff face, and the body came to rest no more than ten feet beneath where they were standing. It seemed unlikely falling only that far would prove lethal, so they agreed the best thing to do was climb down and push him out the rest of the way.

The going was precarious, but when they reached the body they were encouraged to see that the tide was in. They steadied themselves behind it and pushed with their legs with all their might. Because of the noise of the surf they did not hear the body fall into the water. It was too dark to see where it ended up, but at this point, there was really nothing more they could do.

By the time the men drove back for the truck it was long after midnight. Patillo decided to sleep in the job shack, as workmen would start showing up at six. Tade, deeply unaccustomed to the evening's level of physical exertion, drove himself to the Neal Hotel, stumbled up the stairs and collapsed on his bed fully clothed.

CHAPTER 6

Leontine sat motionless at the piano, her hands resting lightly on the ivory keys. She could see her own face reflected in its polished, black surface. Her father had purchased the instrument when she was eight years old, another effort in a long sequence of attempts to find a way to lighten his wife's darkened spirit. As far as Leontine was aware, however, her mother never tried to play it even once.

The late afternoon sun sent rays of light slanting through the window, turning tiny airborne specks into drifting fairy dust she would later wipe from her furniture. With the lightest pressure, she produced a gentle chord. She played another. And another. This was what she wanted to share; this feeling of reverence. This peace. She stopped playing and rested her hands in her lap, acknowledging at last that the time had come to let go of her role as piano teacher.

It wasn't the children. For the most part they were only doing as they were told, with no real need or desire for reverence. She had come across a few in her life, Patrick among them, who had an affinity for music. They sought it out of their own volition and found comfort there, and joy. They had no need for rigid memorization or dread for the tedium of practice. It was a travesty to administer something so beautiful with so much force that it became ugly. She wouldn't do it anymore. No more scenes like the one just ended; an insistent mother demanding that Leontine somehow conjure within her hapless son the desire and ability to create something of which he could not even conceive. Leontine lowered the cover over the piano keys, considering when she would let her roster of students know. She could continue with children who wanted to pursue music for their own reasons – unless that reason was to satisfy someone else's demand. That would not leave many, if any at all.

It was after four o'clock and time to start thinking about the evening meal. She and Daisy shared kitchen duties, though her tenant's irregular hours at the *Daily Independent* dictated that the task fell more often to Leontine. She was happy to do it as she enjoyed cooking, and it was an even trade, to her way of thinking, for the life and companionship Daisy brought into their home.

Leontine headed down the stairs, intending to go inside the market to see if Uncle Remy had set anything aside for her, and also to see if Nicholas Denman had come to collect his son. Just as she reached forward to pull open the door, she was startled by the grinding of the doorbell from the other side. She could see the shape of a man facing the colored glass panels in the top half of her door. She opened it to reveal a teenaged Mexican boy who looked familiar at first glance, though she couldn't quite place him.

"Good afternoon," she said to the boy.

"Leontine, it's me. Juan Carlos."

"Carlito!" she said and opened the door more fully, then reached out her arms for a hug. He squeezed her tightly, then she stepped back to look with amazement into the eyes of the younger brother of her missing fiancé, Vincent Barón.

It had been four years since Vincent headed over the San Marcos Pass along with her father, Francois Birabent, with a delivery of groceries bound for Mattei's Tavern in the Santa Ynez Valley. Ten hours after their departure, her father's body and the fully-loaded wagon arrived at Cold Spring Tavern near the top of the pass, the horses having found the way on their own. Vincent was missing and had not been seen again, and though Leontine searched single-mindedly for anything that might explain what had happened that day, she never found a clue. After two years of fretful searching, she finally succumbed to the pleading of family and friends to give up the quest. She buried her hope in the tomb of her chest and silently waited for it to wither and die.

Leontine ushered Juan Carlos upstairs to the kitchen and offered him some Nabisco Sugar Wafers and milk. He had been only eleven years old at the time of Vincent's disappearance – the same age that Patrick was now. Leontine and Vincent had often included the boy on picnics and outings, and she now felt somewhat chagrined that she had let so much time pass without reaching out to him - though in her own defense, his family rancho was quite far afield, covering territory within the former Ortega Rancho that lay between the mountains and the sea and stretching from El Capitán all the way to Gaviota. She had continued to make the trek for family gatherings for a time, but when it became apparent Vincent was unlikely to turn up, she had allowed ties to sever, as was only right.

"Juan Carlos, I almost can't believe you're here," Leontine said. The boy studied his plate, having yet to take a bite, then he finally looked into Leontine's eyes.

"Something is wrong," he said. "Mama is scared. I think it has something to do with Vincent."

"Why do you think that?"

"I told her again I want to look for him. She yelled at me to leave it alone and made me promise."

"I'm sure she's frightened you might disappear, too," Leontine said. "I would be."

"This is different. I've been talking about it forever and she always said "when you're older, when you're older". But never to leave it alone. Never yelling."

"I'm so sorry. It doesn't sound like Innocencia."

"Something is wrong," he insisted.

"But what can I do?"

"She hides in the house and won't go into town. She doesn't want me to go into town – or even to school. I need to at least go to school."

Leontine looked away, her brow knitted. She found it difficult to take a deep breath.

"You can talk to her. Please. I don't want to ask anyone else."

Leontine felt something engage in her chest, like a wheel set into motion. It was astonishing to sense how easy it would be to pick up the search again, to make herself a slave to hope again – almost as if she had never stopped.

"Oh, Juan Carlos…" she said, intending to disappoint.

"Just think about it," he said hurriedly, as if she could now do anything else. The boy stood to leave. Normally Leontine would have stood with him, but she found herself unable to move.

"Please come. Please."

"All right," Leontine said quietly, knowing the instant she agreed, she was doomed.

It was half an hour later when Patrick came up the stairs to find her still sitting at the kitchen table. He sat across from her and leaned forward with his chest resting against the table and his hands folded between his knees. Leontine observed him wordlessly, her mind not yet engaged.

"Are you sick?" Patrick asked.

Leontine sighed, then seemed to recover herself. She said, "I don't think so. Are you hungry?"

"I don't know. My dad told someone to call the store. He doesn't know when he'll be home. I wonder what he's doing." He meant it to sound off-hand, but even he could hear the nervousness in his own voice.

"I have leftover bread pudding. Let's have that, then go wait at your house," Leontine offered, sensing Patrick's yearning for normalcy and home. She set about starting the fire in the enormous cast iron Majestic stove that dominated her kitchen space. How her father had ever managed to transport and install the heavy appliance in the second-floor apartment she could not even imagine. Her mother had been so proud of the thing, but Leontine sometimes eyed the more modern and easily operated gas and kerosene stoves with longing. She retrieved the pudding from the icebox and placed it inside the oven to re-heat.

Upon finishing the light meal, Leontine left a note for Daisy, then the two headed for the Denmans' cottage on De la Vina Street. The night air was growing moist from another fog bank steadily advancing over the channel toward shore. It pushed the sound of the surf farther inland as well, and one could hear the ceaseless waves in the distance beneath a symphony of crickets. The two were silent, each caught up in their own weighted thoughts as they walked.

Tesla greeted them joyously as soon as they rounded the corner onto De la Vina Street. He had scooted on home at his normal dinner time, only to find nobody at home, poor dear. Once arrived, Leontine went into the kitchen to brew some tea while Patrick fed his dog and his fish. She was still absorbed in the task when Nicholas arrived home.

Patrick rushed to meet his father at the door as soon as he heard his step on the porch. Nicholas was not quite fully inside when Patrick hugged his waist and buried his face in his father's chest. They stood like that for a long moment, saying nothing, until Patrick finally drew in a deep breath, stood back and let his dad come inside.

The cottage felt cozy – thanks in large part to Leontine. The first time she had visited the bachelor-esque home, more than a year ago, bare walls and wood floors had the space feeling cold and austere. As a doctor, Nicholas Denman earned a good living, and it had been joyful fun for her to select rugs, tables, lamps, clocks, pillows and various other adornments, without the restrictions normally imposed by frugality.

Leontine set three teacups on the dining table, including Patrick in the adult activity as if she had always done so. Nicholas went to wash his face and hands as she scrounged up some biscuits from the pantry, arranged them on a dinner plate and carried them to the table, pretending not to notice Patrick alternating the addition of cream and sugar into his cup until any actual tea flavor was sufficiently overwhelmed. Once they all sat down, Patrick meant to give his dad a minute to unwind before he began questioning him about the body, but he found it impossible to wait.

"Do you know what happened to him?" he asked.

Nicholas breathed a cooling breath over his steaming beverage and shook his head. "Not really," he had to admit.

"Was he drowned?" Leontine asked.

"No. His neck is broken and he had no water in his lungs. He must have fallen from the cliff."

Patrick asked, "What happened to his hands?"

"They were burned somehow. Did you see his hands, Son?"

Patrick stared into his already-empty teacup.

"I'm sorry," his father said. He scooted his chair closer to his son and rested his arm on the back of his chair. "That's probably all we need to say about him tonight."

"It's a relief to rule out foul play at least," Leontine said. But something in the doctor's expression made her understand that foul play had not been ruled out at all. They steered the conversation to matters more mundane as the adults finished their tea.

Nicholas assured Leontine he would see to the dishes, followed by an offer to walk her home. When Patrick whistled for Tesla and jumped up to join them she dismissed the faintest whiff of disappointment that she would not be alone with the doctor to probe for more information about the poor victim. She wondered for a moment at the rush of excitement she felt, realizing it harkened back to the previous year and her involvement in helping to sort out a murder that had occurred at the Potter Hotel. Heaven forbid another lethal crime had been committed, but if it had been, perhaps she could be of assistance. If nothing else, it might provide a welcome distraction from the upsetting visit from Juan Carlos.

CHAPTER 7
Saturday, August 21, 1909

The following morning found Daisy in the office of her boss, Tom O'Brien. He held out her typewritten account of the passage of the women's restricted drinking ordinance for her to take back, then let his hand flop to the desk, realizing she had no intention of reaching for it.

"I'm not saying 'no', I'm saying 'not this.'"

Daisy folded her arms across her chest, but turned to face him more squarely, thereby inferring he could say more. Inwardly, O'Brien was amused and, if he admitted it, continually charmed by her outlandish behavior. He thought her funny and brash and generally refreshing when compared with his stable of more well-seasoned, if deadpan, newspapermen. Outwardly, however, he was her boss, and so he adopted what he thought a more appropriate stern demeanor.

"Explain the law. No tirades about temperance," he said and lifted the sheet again. Daisy snatched it out of his hand.

"Tirade. Hardly."

"Leave it out. And why are you covering the council?"

"Fernandez had something else. I volunteered."

O'Brien turned his attention back to the stack of articles and advertisements on his desk awaiting his approval as he waved her out of his office. Daisy lingered, however, until he finally looked up at her again.

"What?" he asked.

"You know who found that body at Castle Rock?"

"Some boy."

"My landlady's friend." Daisy's tone implied she had just played some kind of trump card.

"Reed is already talking to the sheriff."

"I thought I could get something from Patrick – the boy. I think women readers would want to know how the child was affected."

O'Brien leaned back in his chair and studied the eager young woman. He couldn't think of any reason to spoil her fun.

"Don't write a novel about it," he said and waved her out again. Daisy headed quickly for the door, not wanting him to see a somewhat triumphal smile she couldn't quite wipe from her face.

When O'Brien had hired her on a trial basis six months earlier, Daisy's assignment was to provide notices and information primarily for the female readership. She would supply an account of the thinking and planning emanating from the numerous and varied women's club meetings going on about town nearly every day. To her relief, he set her loose on the task without oversight, saying she would no doubt know best which topics women might find of interest. It was a relief because Daisy's interests were much more aligned with events actually unfolding around her, and less so with any thinking about, or planning of, occurrences yet to come. Though she dutifully attended meetings of the Women's Relief Corps, Associated Charities, the Women's Civic League, the Santa Barbara Woman's Club and even, occasionally, the Christian Temperance Union, she spent at least an equal amount of time in local hang outs, at city council meetings, and basically loitering around the sheriff's office attached to the jail behind the courthouse.

She was learning her way around her new boss, and so far it seemed the most fruitful course of action for pursuing what she considered real news, was to simply do whatever she wanted. She knew he was giving her more rope than she probably deserved, and had a suspicion it had more to do with her youth and appearance than any dazzling successes as a journalist. He liked her – a lot. It was increasingly apparent to everyone but himself, but she was adamant that she would not resort to flirting or teasing to receive special treatment, as she assumed that's what her male colleagues expected her to do.

Thomas O'Brien was the managing editor of the *Daily Independent*. One of three primary newspapers in town, the *Independent* was owned by local dignatario, Thomas M. Storke, who took an instant liking to O'Brien and almost immediately began to mentor him as the future boss.

O'Brien was lean and lanky with auburn hair, an impressive mustache and golden-brown eyes that crinkled when he smiled – a relatively rare occurrence. He was a consummate bachelor who, to the consternation of a long list of formerly marriageable maidens, had apparently chosen the *Daily Independent* as his bride. Now thirty-five, it seemed unlikely any girl would ever be able to change his autonomous ways – that is until Daisy Merrie came whooshing into his news room, a whirlwind of enthusiasm and determination. In her presence he understood how dour and crotchety he had become, how disillusioned and tired. If asked, he would have said his attentiveness and support for Daisy sprung from a place of kindred spirit. When approaching mid-life, there can evolve a fervent desire to mentor and pass along one's hard-won knowledge to another generation finding its way along the same path. He thought she had talent and brains, and reminded himself frequently that he was nearly old enough to be her father.

Daisy headed over to her desk. Unlike the *Daily News*, where she had worked for a short time the previous year, the massive printing press and type-setting stations were located in a separate room in the back, apart from the writers and accounting clerk in the smaller central office. Tom O'Brien's office had the windows facing State Street, though a large window in his opposing office wall allowed plenty of daylight into the newsroom. He had the only telephone as well. One wall of the newsroom was completely covered by tall shelves holding reference books, city directories and a photo library. The accounting clerk worked at an elevated desk next to the entrance to the press room, where he sat on a tall stool, filling in ledger books and punching numbers into a Dalton Calculating Machine. Across from the reference library, two more desks flanked the doorway leading to a basement filled with archived issues of the paper that everyone referred to as "the morgue". In the center of the room was the double-sided desk that Daisy shared with Owen Reed.

Reed had been writing for the *Independent* longer than O'Brien had been in charge, and though Daisy's side of the desk was piled with papers, books, pens and, of course, a typewriter, Owen Reed's side was conspicuously barren, on account of him conducting just short of one hundred percent of his business from the short edge of the bar inside the Stafford Saloon.

Daisy tapped her front teeth with her pen as she considered how to proceed. At breakfast, Leontine had shared her concern for Patrick, saying that he seemed quite shaken by the unfortunate incident. She also expressed a suspicion that Dr. Denman's disquiet about the condition of the body hinted at the possibility of wrongdoing. Daisy's reaction had been much the same as Leontine's the evening before, and faced with her tenant's piqued interest, Leontine found herself further divulging the information about meeting the infant son of the victim on the hip of Victoria Ramirez's daughter. Both agreed the entire situation warranted more thought, and perhaps even action, and pledged to take up the topic again later in the day.

Daisy decided she would make quick work of the drinking ordinance report, then round up Leontine, find Patrick, and get her interview. When she showed up at the market at late morning, she found Leontine behind the counter leaning chin-in-hand and staring idly through the front doors. It registered with Daisy that her friend seemed even more subdued than usual, and she attributed the mood to the concern she no doubt felt for Patrick. Daisy offered a 'good morning' to Uncle Remy who was reading on his stool. He lifted his pipe in greeting without looking up.

"I get to interview Patrick for the paper," Daisy chirped, but her smile faded when she saw Leontine's brow crease.

"I don't know that he'll talk about it. He was having a hard time yesterday."

"Do you think I should wait?"

"You should check with Nicholas at least. He was very protective of Patrick last night."

"Maybe I could interview Nicholas."

Leontine placed a call to the doctor's home number, but after several rings deduced that father and son were not at home.

"Let's go see where the body was found," Daisy said, "and check at the adobe on the way."

It was just the distraction Leontine needed. She was finding it difficult to keep her mind off of the visit from Juan Carlos Barón, and was in serious danger of moping. She needed to get busy with something. She went upstairs and changed into her chocolate brown corduroy skirt, white cotton shirt and matching fitted jacket. She laced up her sturdiest high-topped walking shoes, then securely tied her sun hat into place. Daisy eschewed hats, as evidenced by her suntanned cheeks and sun-bleached chestnut hair, and most often would secure her Gibson Girl hairstyle in place with a broad bow in the same color as whatever skirt she was wearing. Today they were navy blue.

When the women approached the adobe, Tesla trotted out to welcome them, dipping his head with excitement and seeming to smile. They found Nicholas and Patrick hard at work building shelving from bricks and boards that would line the wall of the once-kitchen between the darkroom and the long plank table, now so overloaded with projects and artifacts there was no room to work. Leontine could see the positive effect of the physical labor combined with time spent with his father. Patrick seemed much more himself. As he filled Leontine in on the organizational plan, Daisy quietly asked Nicholas how he thought his son might respond to the idea of an interview.

"I wonder that myself," Nicholas said.

Daisy turned to her young friend. "O'Brien wants me to interview you for the paper."

"Why?"

"A lot of people know something happened at the beach yesterday. We should tell them what we know, even if it's not much so far."

Patrick became purposefully absorbed in the task of sorting items on his table for transfer to the new shelves.

"We're on our way to Castle Rock," Daisy tempted. Still no response. The three adults shared a concerned a look.

"The sheriff has been all over it," Nicholas said, "but he couldn't find any clues."

"He didn't fall there," Patrick said without looking up from his task. The other three turned to face him. "Or if he did, somebody had to drag him to the other side of the rock. It's too far from the water."

"Are you sure?" Daisy asked. Patrick glanced up, his expression communicating that, of course, he was sure.

Leontine asked, "Does the sheriff know that?"

"I don't know," Nicholas said. A sidelong glance communicated his desire to rush down to the beachfront with the women, roll up their collective sleeves, and get to helping uncover whatever events had led to the lawyer floating in the surf.

"I'm going," Daisy said. It was then wordlessly agreed that Leontine would join Daisy in sizing up the scene at the beach, and that Nicholas would stay behind to focus on helping his son somehow regain his equilibrium.

The women took the trolley to the Plaza, skirted the fountain area, and headed for the sand and the path to Castle Rock. They shielded their eyes from the afternoon sun and squinted closely at their surroundings, but neither could recognize anything out of the ordinary. They also searched for any indication that something had been dragged across the sand as Patrick suggested - and quite possibly things had been, but footprints, scrapings and diggings left by subsequent visitors to the popular site made individual markings impossible to discern.

As they scoured the area for clues, Leontine looked up to see a man who appeared to be watching them from the top of the cliff. When he realized she was looking up at him, he shielded his eyes and gazed out over the ocean as if taking in the view. Leontine motioned to Daisy and directed her gaze toward the man. There was little doubt he was monitoring their activity. He was too far away to recognize, and his brown sack suit so commonplace it made him indistinguishable from the great majority of men around town. He held his hat in one hand, and the sun shining through his thick mane of unruly blonde hair created the illusion of a glowing halo. The women continued poking around the rock, keeping a sideways eye on the man watching, mostly just wondering how long he would stay there. It seemed quite a long time until he finally turned away and disappeared from view.

As soon as he vanished, Leontine and Daisy hurried back through the Plaza, then trudged up the road leading to the Leadbetter mansion. They followed the tree-lined path out to the point overlooking Castle Rock where the man had been standing, but when they arrived there wasn't much to see. Neither of them was schooled in recognizing signs of disturbance in a natural environment. There were plenty of footprints and imprints from horse hooves, wagon wheels and even a motor car, but how was one to know how recently marks had been made? And what would one do with the knowledge, once obtained?

"I'm going to see the sheriff," Daisy said. "I can try to find out what he knows so far. And we should probably tell him about that man."

Leontine replied, "I think I'll go see Victoria. She's working on a project for me anyway, and maybe she will have learned something from

Margarita." The women's eyes met and neither could suppress a grin. It was enlivening, this desire to puzzle and pursue and unravel. Most exhilarating.

CHAPTER 8

E. J. Stambach was young and strong with beefy arms, a square jaw and a thick mane of curly blonde hair. He was a fairly recent transplant to Santa Barbara, having moved with his wife and three children from Visalia, California the previous summer. He had been employed for a number of years at the Kaweah Hydro Plant located in the foothills of the Sierra Nevada mountains since its inception in 1899, when he was just sixteen.

Around the turn of the century, separately evolving hydro-electric facilities were beginning to merge as distribution systems improved and the need for electricity multiplied exponentially across the state of California. Several such facilities in central California joined with the ever-expanding Southern California Edison Company, Visalia Electric Light and the Santa Barbara Electric Light Company among them.

When E. J. learned that the newly incorporated Edison Company in Santa Barbara was in need of a manager, he saw opportunity for a new beginning. The installation work he did for Kaweah Hydro was grueling and physically demanding, and though he was now only twenty-six, he could already feel the toll taken on his body. Moreover, he would sometimes be away from home toiling in the Sierra Nevada mountain range for months at a time. His youngest son bore little resemblance to his two older brothers, and E. J. harbored a dark suspicion about his parentage. He was eager for a new situation that might keep him closer to home, and it would be a bonus to supplant his wife into surroundings not quite so familiar.

He had no way of knowing how little his experience with installing equipment for the transmission and distribution of electricity would help him as a budding entrepreneur. Though his knowledge of electrical transmission was impressive, he had no experience whatsoever in sales or business management. In competition with the more established Nielsen-Smith Electric Company, which enjoyed preferential treatment from the city electrician, local residents and businesses, he was finding it difficult to provide for his family.

Francis Fordyce had contacted both Stambach and his counterpart at Nielsen-Smith when seeking to secure an electric company to perform the ill-defined and potentially time-consuming implementation of the experimental trolley project. Anemic compensation for the initial work was leveraged against the promise of a huge payoff if the venture emerged successful. Nielsen-Smith declined immediately. The company was functioning well with no need to pursue inflated returns for taking on risk. Stambach on the other hand, was eager for the chance, and in fact was performing the lion's share of work himself to avoid paying wages and thereby hold onto as much of the three-hundred-dollar contract as possible. He had invested additional time and effort in schooling himself about electrical matters specific to trolley systems – though not all applied because of the lack of rails. The double overhead wiring structure being installed was still largely experimental.

When E. J. showed up at the jobsite on Friday morning, he had an uneasy sense that something was wrong. He had arrived early in order to prepare for the next experiment from a long list of stress tests designed for the trolley car. The workmen had built a "mud bog", an area near the laguna created to simulate the result of a flood and debris flow. The car should be able to plow right through the mess. Just outside the car he noticed footprints and other markings in the mud that indicated there had been quite a lot of activity right next to the trolley car the night before. He saw also that the pole used to connect the car to the overhead wire was already in place, not pulled away from the wire for safety as he was absolutely certain he had left it. He then searched out Patillo, and asked if someone from the golf game had been messing around with the trolley car or something, but Patillo dismissed the question out of hand and grumbled to Stambach to just get back out there and get ready.

It was when he was making his way back to the mud bog that E.J. spotted a stylish Derby hat laying in the scrub brush near the debris flow. He picked it up to inspect more closely, hoping for some kind of distinguishing marking so that its owner might be located. To his alarm, he found that the inside rim of the hat was singed. He raised the derby to his own face, catching the unmistakable scent of burnt hair, and he carried it to the trolley car with mounting anxiety. He'd had the misfortune of witnessing similar evidence of electrocution more than once while installing wire in the Sierras. He mounted the trolley car and examined the handle of the electrical pole to see if there was any evidence of burned flesh, but it was clean. He looked again at the suggestion of activity in the mud surrounding the car, then scowled deeply in the direction of the clubhouse. Nothing good had happened here, of that he was certain. He jumped from the trolley and waded through the bog over to his horse, then stuffed the burned hat into his saddlebag. He knew he should probably hand it over to Patillo, but something about the way he had avoided the whole topic earlier had put E. J. on guard.

The mud bog test went well, the heavy trolley car zipping through the miring mess with power and ease, so it was barely past noon when he left the jobsite for his office. He ducked into the Stafford Saloon for a sandwich and a beer before going back to his office, and it was there that he learned about the dead body found on the beach earlier in the day. The information only served to increase his unease, and after making a stop at his office, he headed down to Castle Rock to have a look around.

He couldn't find anything revealing down by the rock itself, and so headed up to the cliff above so he could get a broader view. It was then that he saw two women poking around as he had been doing just a few minutes earlier, and he recognized one of the women as an employee of the *Daily Independent* whose offices were right next door to his own office. He briefly considered approaching the women. In the end, however, he decided to get back to work, but to keep his eyes and ears open.

CHAPTER 9

Caroline Fordyce sat behind the library desk, now properly dressed in a black velvet mourning gown. The stand-up neckline parted at her delicate throat which drew the eye downward along a trail of thirty velvet-covered buttons, a gentle flare of the luscious material accentuating her tiny waist. The ensemble included a black velvet Tudor beret hat, its customary feather replaced by a black lace veil that, at the moment, trailed down her back, but could be placed over her face should the need for concealment arise.

The fire in the fireplace had been dampened and one of the windows opened to allow in a bit of a freshening ocean breeze. Three bound sets of papers lay on the leather desk blotter before her. It had taken no time at all to locate the documents, as she continually kept herself informed about the whereabouts of any information her late husband considered important. The papers had changed everything. The challenge now would be to somehow keep Margaret ignorant of the fact that their purposes were no longer aligned. Caroline had to consider what her course of action might be should her husband's assistant sense the change in the wind.

Caroline brushed a finger lightly over the top page of one set of documents. She could feel the oil from the carbonated paper as she traced Francis' name, inserted beneath the words "Last Will and Testament". It was not surprising that Francis did not keep the original type-written manuscripts with him, and she assumed they were locked in his office in Los Angeles. Pity.

There were two wills actually, and adoption papers for Frankie. None of the copies in hand were fully witnessed or signed. A carbonized copy of her signature appeared at the bottom of the adoption papers, along with that of Francis, but Margarita Ramirez had yet to sign. Without signatures, none of the documents were binding, but she hoped they might prove useful nonetheless.

When Caroline first read the wills the previous evening, she was devastated. One left the sum total of Fordyce's considerable personal fortune to Francis Fordyce, III, as would be expected. What was not expected was the other will, which one had to assume was the governing text until the adoption papers were made official. It bestowed the fortune to Winnie – Winifred Fordyce – to whom Francis had been married for nearly thirty years. Caroline had been passed over entirely. The discovery hurt her deeply and she suffered tearfully for several wretched hours. But it was not as if a true love was lost, and soon enough the disregard she felt turned bitter. It had never been spoken aloud, but the implicit bargain struck with Francis years earlier had been clear to her way of thinking – a life of luxury in return for an heir.

Caroline had become acquainted with Francis on a week-long yachting excursion to Catalina Island with her aunt and uncle. Winnie Fordyce spent most of the trip battling sea sickness and gout, and Caroline learned from the oft-inebriated lawyer that his aging and ailing wife had been a disappointment to him in nearly every regard, but especially egregious had been her inability to bear him a son. He was now quite obsessed with the situation, and by the end of the week it was all but decided that Fordyce would divorce himself from his increasing dissatisfaction and attempt procreation with a new young bride who might finally be able to provide him with his heart's desire.

Though scarcely more than a child herself, Caroline was sufficiently self-aware to suspect that her future happiness would more likely be found in the trappings of prosperity than the starry-eyed devotion of some young man. Francis was more than thirty years her senior, and though his hair was gray and his middle thickening, she was not repulsed by him in the slightest. She decided then and there that this lawyer would suit nicely, and accepted his heartfelt, if somewhat spontaneous, proposal of marriage. The ensuing divorce had been civilized, no doubt because Winnie was allowed to keep the residence in Pasadena, her membership in the Los Angeles Country Club and enough capital to live out her remaining years in comfort.

It never occurred to Francis that he could be the one lacking reproductive vigor, but after more than a year of efforting with his new young wife, it had to be acknowledged, that might well be the case. It was then that his law clerk, Margaret Ramirez, learned that a colossal lapse in judgment had left her in a family way. Furious with herself and asserting that she wanted nothing to do with the offspring of her married lover, Margaret confided in her boss, hoping he might assist in finding a good home for the child and, more importantly, allow her to keep her job. To her relief and surprise, he offered to adopt the baby himself – provided it was male – in exchange for more money than she would no doubt earn in her entire career. It was agreed that Margaret and Caroline would retreat to his residence in San Francisco where the baby would be born. If a girl, Francis would do all he could to secure some pleasing situation for her there. If it was a boy, Margaret would nurse and care for him with Caroline's assistance for several months, after which time they would return to Los Angeles and pass the baby off as the natural offspring of Francis and Caroline Fordyce. How naive they had all been.

As Francis carried on with his practice in Los Angeles, he was, for the most part, unaware of the deepening dislike Caroline and Margaret harbored for one another. Caroline thought Margaret a backwater heathen, an ignorant woman whatever her education, and without question, morally bankrupt. Margaret found Caroline self-absorbed, pretentious and childish in the extreme. Only her own self-loathing and abhorrence of the child growing inside her, kept her from abandoning the whole idea despite the potential financial gain.

That was before she experienced the tidal wave that is biology. An avalanche of hormones, evolving sensations deep in her womb and the agony of childbirth culminated in the featherlike grasp of a tiny hand that left her helpless with love and fierce with protectiveness. It was a complete change of heart and mind. She swam in the liquid depths of Frankie's eyes as he clung to her and drew life from her breast and it was only a matter of days before she realized, there was no way on earth she would ever put her son in the care of the ridiculous wife of Francis Fordyce. She did not know how, but she would extricate herself from the promises already made, and somehow raise her child on her own, or perhaps put him up for a normal adoption with at least a chance of ending up with a suitable mother.

Several weeks after the birth of Frankie, Caroline reached a similar conclusion. She had experienced no hormonal changes or bonding interactions. She saw only a leaking, squalling mess, and the last thing she wanted to do was be in the same room with it, never mind imagining herself up to her elbows in its debris. The women had set aside their harsh judgments of one another and discussed how best to bring Francis on board with their shared revelation – the adoption must be abandoned.

Sadly, Francis was determined that the child be his. He was overjoyed that genetics had seemingly ignored Margaret's Mexican heritage in favor of the northern European lineage of the father, making Francis all the more resolute. He convinced the women to join him in Santa Barbara in an effort to find common ground, and he rented the most extravagant and appealing dwelling he could find in order to see if they could all just settle down and find a way to ease into the situation.

But now the train was decidedly off the rails. Caroline and Margaret had sworn to each other that the adoption papers would never be signed, no matter what enticements Francis might conjure up. Were that to happen now, Winifred Fordyce would make a clean sweep. If Caroline was actually mother to the child, however, she would remain in her elevated station, a tender widow and caretaker to the young lord of the manor. She gathered the documents and slid them into the desk drawer in case they were needed, then squared her shoulders, faced the door, and waited for Margaret Ramirez to join her and at last have a conversation about the recent sequence of most unfortunate events.

Margarita always dressed with the most current trend, and she appeared now in a tailored and viciously-corseted drape-front suit. Frilly adornments attached to a white lace blouse worn under a tightly-fitted suit jacket and ballooned out from her chest. That, combined with a heavily festooned hat perched sideways on her head, conjured up the image of a young robin redbreast playing at dress-up.

Caroline motioned her to the facing leather desk chair. The gesture seemed commanding and presumptuous to Margaret, and so she chose to stand. "What do you want?" she asked.

"Obviously, we need to discuss what's happened."

"I'm sure you have a lot to deal with. We'll be out of your way as soon as possible."

"I think you should stay here."

"Whatever for?"

"Just until everything is cleared up."

"It's really none of my business now. But I wish you luck." Margaret said, turning toward the door.

In a fit of desperation, Caroline blurted out the truth, "I need you to sign the adoption papers. It's the only way for me to inherit."

Margaret stopped and faced Caroline again.

"I won't get in your way," Caroline continued. "You can do whatever you want. Although it would probably be best if we continue to live under the same roof."

"I see. I would be your nanny I suppose."

"That would make the most sense."

Margarita shook her head. She didn't have to consider for two seconds which atmosphere would be best for her son; the cold austerity surrounding Caroline Fordyce, or the familial embrace of the Ramirez clan.

"No," she replied and left the room.

"It's better for everyone," Caroline called after her – to no response.

CHAPTER 10

Daisy rounded the corner onto Caesar's Alley to cut through City Hall Plaza on her way to the sheriff's office near the courthouse. She was following the young man ahead of her and had been for two blocks. She had known instantly who he was without having to see his face – her own brother, Will. She observed as he approached the *Daily News* across the street from the Raffour Hotel, noting with a stab of remorse, that his clothes appeared limp and stained, his boots cracked and scuffed. He paused for a moment, adjusted his wool flat-cap, then lifted his chin and stepped purposefully inside the newspaper office.

Daisy ducked around the corner of the Raffour and stared sightlessly for several moments as she let out a long, controlled breath. Two minutes later she heard footsteps returning toward State Street. She hesitated, overrun with two powerful and opposing impulses at once: to leap into her younger brother's path and throw her arms around him, and to stay right where she was, out of sight. When she was sure he had moved past where he could see her, she stepped into the street again to watch him walk away. He turned right onto State Street, presumably on his way to the *Daily Independent*.

Daisy had forgotten what she was about for a moment and looked around, trying to remember the task at hand. Ah, yes. Sheriff Stewart and the body at the beach. She would think about her brother later she told herself, which naturally turned out to be impossible.

Daisy continued up Anacapa Street toward the sheriff's office and tried to fend off the troubling thoughts now invading her mind. Of course, this was bound to happen sooner or later, she thought, reminding herself that it wasn't as though she had never imagined the day when someone from the family might come looking for her. But now that it was happening, she realized she neglected to ever imagine what she should do when it happened. She went over the roster of her siblings in her mind. She, herself was about to turn twenty. That would make Will seventeen, so Violet was fifteen, Rose was eleven, Iris eight, Lilly five, and Junior must already be two. And then there was The Baby. Daisy had bolted before learning the name or sex of her father's little bastard.

The Baby was the final straw. Since she was a child of three, Daisy had played some version of both mother and father to the endlessly expanding horde of her parents' children. Her father worked hard at the docks, she'd give him that. And he gave Daisy most of the money he earned, to spend on their dilapidated shack and the pile of progeny. He drank plenty, too, for the most part accomplishing his nightly stupor via payment of sorts from fellow revelers. He was rewarded, in a sense, simply for being the life of the party.

Her mother took care of an elderly and infirm matron on Octavia Street. She resided in the woman's mansion during the week, only returning home between noon on Saturday and six o'clock on Sunday evenings. It was just long enough to do her own laundry, re-acquaint herself with her brood, then breed again if her husband happened to be around at the same time.

Both of her parents had been there on the day Daisy left. She was standing in the kitchen, red-faced and burning with resentment as the bouquet of little sisters clamored for their mother's brief attention. Her mother was doting on Junior who, at the time, was not yet walking. Daisy heard the front door open and then her father's voice - then a baby's cry. She walked into the living room where all were silent and gaping at her father and a squalling newborn. She only heard the tail end of her father's explanation, but it was enough. He was holding the baby out to his wife, saying, "She ain't even got a regular place to live. She left it at the office with a note. I don't know what to do."

Daisy turned wide-eyed to face her mother. Did he expect her to reach for some other woman's baby? Attempting to read her mother's expression, Daisy abruptly realized that the baby was also his. She whirled on her father, hating him in that moment, and intending to banish him and his illicit offspring from the family hearth. But before she could make a sound she heard her mother speak behind her.

"Give it here," she said. Daisy turned on her instead.

"What?! You are not touching that baby," Daisy hurled at her mother, and she put herself in-between her parents. "Get it out of here!" she screamed at her father. "Get out!"

Her father looked pathetic and sheepish. He spoke to his daughter, but kept pleading eyes on his wife. "This ain't your business, Daisy," he said. "Flora, I'll make it up to you – " but Daisy cut him off.

"Not my business!" Who did he think was taking care of all his kids? She looked at her mother, whose expression was much the same as that of her husband, communicating clearly that Daisy should butt out.

Her mother reached for the infant saying, "Eight is not eight times the work."

"*How would you know?!*" Daisy shrieked. Horrified, she looked back and forth between her chagrined father and her spiritless mother, and let the reality sink in. Junior would be in diapers for another year at least, and Lilly wasn't quite done with them yet. Three in diapers – and four more besides. Something broke inside – she actually felt it come apart in her chest – and she calmly left the room without another word to anyone.

It took roughly a quarter hour for Daisy to collect her belongings. She was at the train station within the hour, and in another twenty-four was standing on the stoop of her soon-to-be landlady, Leontine Birabent. She had not corresponded with anyone in her family since that moment. In a way, it was as if the entire scene was frozen in time. Surprisingly, she had not thought overly much about it, and because she had not, none of the ravaged emotional terrain had been reclaimed. Before she knew it, she was in tears, aching with longing for the brothers and sisters that had been her entire life until the day she stormed out. It was in this sorry condition that Nat Stewart found her in front of his office.

Sheriff Stewart was just returning from a trek to Hope Ranch. When he had returned to his office after scouring the Castle Rock area that morning, young Pimiento Morales and his mother were awaiting his arrival. The sheriff needed a lot more work on his Spanish, and the Morales family was no more proficient in English, but he believed the two were asking him what had become of a dead body the boy stepped on out at the Potter Country Club the night before last. Sheriff Stewart had heard nothing of any of it. The only dead body to show up recently was the one at Castle Rock. He asked if the fellow might have been drunk. Mother and son communicated that Pimi's boss, Sr. Patillo, had tried to tell Pimi that very thing this morning, but the boy was adamant. The man had been unquestionably, thoroughly dead.

"What did he look like? Uh – *qué expresión?*" Stewart asked pointing to his own face.

The boy seemed uncertain. He glanced at his mother, then back to the sheriff, tilted his head to the side and rolled his eyes back, his tongue poking from the corner of his mouth. The sheriff squelched an inappropriate smile and said, "No – uh...*que aspecto? Cuantos años?*

"*No sé. Viejo. Rico.*"

"Old and rich," Stewart repeated, mostly to himself. He suspected the child had a much different perspective from his own on both counts. Then he said, "Okay, I'll look into it. Okay...*gracias.*"

He didn't know what else to say. He wrote down the address of the Morales family on East Ortega Street, should he need to contact them again, tipped his hat to Mrs. Morales, and shook young Pimi's hand in parting. He then went inside his office to think about it, but before he even sat down he turned and marched right back out to where Lois was tethered, swung into the saddle and headed out to Hope Ranch. This was the third time someone had mentioned the Potter Country Club since the body washed up at Castle Rock. It felt like he should pay the place a visit.

The sheriff had attended the grand opening of the country club the preceding March, but there had been no reason to return until today. Any conflicts arising during the course of fine dining, golf, polo and picnicking had thus far not required the intervention of law enforcement. The hard-packed dirt of Hubbard Avenue bore evidence of more automobile traffic than most roads in town, no doubt because guests of the Potter Hotel were transferred to and from the country club several times a day via the Potter motorbus, rather than by horse or carriage. To his left, Laguna Blanca reflected the morning sun, and the sheriff shielded his eyes from the glare as he perused his surroundings.

He recalled the gentle grassy slope between the clubhouse and the lake, and the rolling pastoral land dotted with scrub oak trees leading out to the Pacific that he had seen on his previous visit. He tried to reconcile that vision with what surrounded him now. Though it was

Saturday, the trackless trolley prototype was crawling with workmen. Nearly the entire space below the country club by the lake had been impacted to some degree. He halted Lois in the shade of an oak tree and observed workmen engaged in the most curious undertakings. No matter how he studied the scene, he just couldn't quite get a sense of what was going on. It appeared that the task at hand was to undermine work already accomplished. One group of men worked to drag rocks, branches and even bales of hay to block a broad section of the graded track, while others farther along the route laboriously extended a trench running from the lake to the road that would ultimately submerge the very thing they had created in the first place. Meanwhile, he could see several workmen in the distance transporting soil with wheelbarrows with the obvious intention of manufacturing a giant mound where a scraping machine had only just leveled the situation out. In the middle of the mess stood a job shack, a sign affixed to the door informing that James Patillo was the man in charge.

Stewart walked Lois over to the shack and dismounted. He tried the door but found it locked, and a peek in the single grime-covered window revealed no one inside. He climbed back onto his horse and wandered around the area, sensing more than seeing the eyes of the workmen silently following his progress, no doubt wary of the badge on his chest. When he approached the group digging the trench to ask if anybody knew where he might find Mr. Patillo, they obligingly looked around and reported that the man was not in sight at the moment, but if the sheriff cared to stick around they were sure he would reappear. Stewart asked the men if any of them knew Pimiento Morales, and they all did. The boy had been around that morning, but none of them knew where he was now.

The sheriff definitely wanted to have a chat with Mr. Patillo at some point, but decided to head back into town for the moment. He needed to focus on the Castle Rock business and would follow up on the report from young Mr. Morales after he figured out what had happened to the lawyer. If signs directed him back out to Hope Ranch again in the course of that investigation, he would try harder to find Mr. Patillo.

Patillo meanwhile, was watching Sheriff Stewart ride away from his hiding place inside the job shack. As soon as the lawman was out of site, he left the shack and trudged up the hill to the clubhouse to send another message to Tade.

☙ ☙ ☙

Daisy heard Sheriff Stewart talking softly to Lois as he tethered her to the hitching post. She had a couple of minutes to swipe at her tears and smooth her hair before he rounded the corner to head into his office. A good, hard cry takes as long as it will, however, and to her dismay, she responded to his fond greeting with a trembling lower lip and more tears. Surprised beyond words at this reception from the normally-buoyant Miss Merrie, the sheriff, a husband and father to two daughters, instinctively offered his shoulder for a dousing. Once it seemed Daisy had the waterworks in check he opened the door and guided her gently inside to find out what in the world might be the matter.

"My brother is here – I saw him on the street. I don't know what I'm going to do about that, but it's not the reason I'm here."

"Okay." The sheriff did what he did best; he sat back to listen.

"Leontine and I went to have a look at Castle Rock." She glanced at the sheriff, only now considering he might be annoyed. She saw nothing in his expression to give her pause.

"We were looking for clues. Nicholas said the man must have fallen from the cliff because his neck was broken, but Patrick said if he did fall, he wouldn't have ended up on the other side of Castle Rock."

The sheriff had spent time enough with Patrick Denman to know better than to discount anything the boy might say, especially given his undeniable help in the solving of a murder at the Potter Hotel the preceding year.

"While we were investigating, we saw a man up on the bluffs watching us. He seemed very suspicious."

"That's interesting."

"I know," Daisy agreed, picking up steam as the relating of events pushed her own family business farther into the background. "There's something strange going on. Leontine is with Victoria Ramirez now. Her daughter worked for Mr. Fordyce."

"We've met."

"Do tell," Daisy encouraged, but the sheriff remained silent.

"Patrick has already figured some things out, but he's very upset since finding the body," she continued. "I think we should all meet and compare notes. You know, the five of us." And then there came that grin, the same one she and Leontine had been unable to suppress earlier, and it appeared on the sheriff's face as well.

"Potter dining room at 6:00," Stewart said. "But what about your brother?"

Daisy sighed. "He'll find me eventually."

When Leontine arrived at Victoria's studio, she found her friend at her patio table nursing a cup of coffee and idly watching the chickens scratch in the yard. Witnessing the uncharacteristic gloominess, Leontine felt chagrined that the original intent for her visit had been nothing more than an attempt to ferret information, and she abandoned the course of action immediately. She moved a cushioned wrought-iron chair closer to Victoria and sat beside her. They watched the chickens in silence for several minutes, and Leontine could hear Bebé, Bombón and Gruñon snorting and horsing around in the corral. At last, Victoria heaved a big sigh and the women's eyes met.

"I am forbidden to speak," Victoria said.

"I understand," Leontine replied, though she didn't really. She took Victoria's hand. If the strength of their relationship could be demonstrated in the depth of their confidence, perhaps Leontine could be first to confide. Victoria had, after all, stood by her through the years of obsession after the Death and Disappearance. It was when Victoria's voice joined the chorus of those begging for Leontine to set the searching aside and move on with her life, that she had given it up at last.

"I was paid a visit by Juan Carlos," Leontine began. She saw surprise immediately followed by concern on Victoria's face.

"*Pobrecito,*" Victoria murmured. Leontine was uncertain if the empathy was for herself or for Juan Carlos.

"He's dreadfully worried. He said something is wrong with Innocencia and asked me to go out and see her." Leontine searched her friend's eyes and found herself holding her breath.

"Then go," Victoria said, without hesitation. Leontine was taken aback. It was not the advice she expected – or wanted.

"But he wants to try to find out about Vincent."

"Of course."

"I don't think I can - " Leontine wasn't even sure what it was she felt she could not do. Victoria surprised her then by standing, fueled by a sudden rush of anger.

"We must help each other, *mija*. Why would God provide us with family if he means for us to struggle alone? Carlito is a child. Will you turn your back to a child?"

With that, Victoria burst into tears, excused herself, then went inside her studio. Leontine blinked in surprise, feeling scolded and bruised. She waited for a bit, nursing hurt feelings and half-expecting Victoria to come back out and apologize. When it appeared that would not be the case, she finally rose from her chair and headed back home.

CHAPTER 11

Six o'clock found Leontine, Daisy, Patrick and Nicholas arrived at the Potter Hotel dining room. Leontine appeared sleek and stylish in a deep forest-green chiffon dress with a wide fitted waist panel, full skirt and short train, and matching hat with chiffon bows and ruffling. Daisy looked adorable in Leontine's sky-blue beaded dinner dress with an empire waist and sheer insert at the low squared neckline, embroidered with clusters of flowers in pink, rose and lime green. The bejeweled hair pins she wore in lieu of a hat matched the embroidery in color and theme.

The four were informed that their customary table was currently occupied. With no need for consultation, Nicholas informed the maître d' that they preferred to wait for that particular table to become free. In any case, the sheriff had yet to arrive, so they went out to the sunporch to wait.

Leontine observed that the rousing sense of purpose the adults shared, apparently did not extend to Patrick. He moved a short distance away and slid onto a wooden rocking chair. He appeared stiff and uncomfortable in his good suit with long pants. His father had managed to get his hair under control by parting it crisply on one side, then plastering it in place with pomade. Patrick's gaze was anchored in the direction of Stearns Wharf, and several times he pushed his glasses up on his nose, though they had not moved. He appeared determined to avoid looking in the direction of Castle Rock. There was no question in Leontine's mind that he was still deeply traumatized, and she wondered yet again how she might help put his mind at ease.

Daisy took the opportunity to get some general information from the doctor for the story she would write for the Sunday edition about what was known about the unfortunate incident at Castle Rock thus far.

She expressed her desire to tell it from Patrick's point of view. Though concerned, he ultimately gave permission to name Patrick as the one who had stumbled upon the body.

As they spoke, Leontine went and sat in the rocker next to Patrick. He glanced at her in acknowledgement, then resumed staring at the wharf. Leontine searched her mind for something to say that might strike just the right tone of lightheartedness, or at the very least normalcy. Their silence was uncharacteristically awkward for several moments, until they sighed, nearly in unison, and a measure of peace returned. They kept their eyes eastward until the maître d' came to tell them their table was ready.

A cheerful waiter had already delivered a tureen of exquisite cream of potato soup, and a covered basket of fresh bread still warm from the ovens, when Sheriff Stewart hurried into the dining room. Nicholas ladled portions into each bowl and they circled the bread basket as the sheriff explained what had delayed his arrival.

Following his conversation with Daisy, and mulling over Patrick's suggestion that the body most likely did not start out where it was found, he decided to pay another visit to Pimi Morales and pose a few more questions. The boy's ten-year-old sister, Maria Luisa, a fourth-grader at Lincoln School, knew plenty of English, and served quite handily as interpreter. The sheriff coaxed several details out of Pimi, who seemed to enjoy recounting the incident for his little sister and so appear brave and strong in her eyes. He remembered that the man had been wearing a suit, waistcoat and tie but no hat. He described the men who had come running to his aid: his boss Sr. Patillo, Sr. Ramirez who had taken them home in the carriage rented from the Tally Ho stables, and another businessman who came running from his motorcar.

The sheriff asked him again what his boss had said about the man being drunk. He asked if the carriage driver or the man from the car had suggested the victim might be dead, but Pimi did not speak with the businessman, and Sr. Ramirez had been careful to talk about anything else. Stewart asked once more if there was any chance that the man had been alive, but the boy stood his ground. Despite whatever his boss had told him, Pimi knew better. Dead is dead and there is no mistaking it.

The sheriff returned to his office to consult the street directory to learn the location of Santa Barbara Paving Company, with the intention of showing up there on Monday if he was unable to locate Mr. Patillo the following day. He also placed a call to the Tally Ho Stables to see if he could have a conversation with Mr. Ramirez. As it turned out, Justito had informed his cousin Diego of his decision to deliver the distressed boy and his mother home from the country club when Mr. Fordyce did not show up for his contracted ride. The sheriff learned that it was Margarita Ramirez, in her capacity as Mr. Fordyce's assistant, who had arranged for the carriage. Stewart asked Diego for Justito's address so he could get a first-hand account, but there was already no question in his mind that the man the boy stumbled over in Hope Ranch and the lawyer washed up on the beach at Castle Rock were one and the same – Francis Fordyce. It was also worth noting that the Ramirez name kept popping up. When he finished his tale, the sheriff asked what the others thought and then gratefully turned his attention to his soup.

Leontine said, "I have known Justito and Margarita since they were children. It's impossible to imagine they are involved in anything sordid."

"Nearly anyone can be a victim of circumstance," Dr. Denman observed. "They may be caught up in something outside of their control."

"Why would someone move the body?" Daisy asked.

The sheriff replied, "Either they wanted it found at Castle Rock or they did not want it found in that mess of whatever it is they're building out there. Does anyone know what that's all about?"

Although all three local papers had, at some point, made mention of the project, the stories were light on information. The situation was so far outside of town it failed to garner much interest in Santa Barbara proper.

Daisy, who had thought to bring a notepad and pen - as she nearly always did - decided to rely on a technique she devised when looking into the murder at the Potter Hotel during the visit of the Great White Fleet. She would make a list of the names of all the people they were aware of that had any association with the death of the lawyer. They each called out names as they occurred to them, and in the end the list included: Pimi Morales and his mother, Margarita Ramirez and her brother Justito, Caroline Fordyce, Mr. Patillo, and the man in the motorcar whose name they did not know. For good measure, she added the mysterious man who had spied on her and Leontine from above Castle Rock.

"I want to find out more about what it is they're building," Daisy said.

"If that's where the man was killed, it could have something to do with it."

Dr. Denman said, "Nobody has said he was killed."

"I want to talk to this Patillo. It looks like he lied to his worker and I'd like to know why he thought he needed to do that," the sheriff said.

As the others planned their next moves, Leontine was quiet. She had silently come to the conclusion that she must, for the moment, turn her attention elsewhere.

"I'm quite certain my friend Victoria has information about her children she feels she cannot disclose," she said. "I could try to talk to her about it, but not until Tuesday evening. I'm traveling to Gaviota tomorrow and will not return until Tuesday afternoon."

Daisy was surprised, this being the first she heard of the traveling plans. "Is everything all right?"

"Of course," Leontine said, though she doubted it was true. "Just a visit to my cousins at Arroyo Hondo," wondering when she said it why she was bothering to lie.

"Can I come?" Patrick asked.

"Patrick," Nicholas cautioned, intending to school him in the lack of etiquette displayed in inviting himself along.

"I would appreciate the company." Leontine felt certain the trip would be good for him. Nicholas did not immediately assent, and Leontine could sense a moment of tension between father and son. They locked eyes, silent communication flowing between them.

"I'd rather go with Lulubelle," Patrick said, using her father's nickname for her.

"Besides, the carnival starts Tuesday," Nicolas said. The two-day event was sponsored by the Civic League and officially marked the end of summer. Students would reacquaint themselves with each other and their teachers prior to the start of a new school year. Alameda Park was to be transformed. There would be games, contests, exhibitions, recitals, plenty of snacks and free ice-cream.

"I don't care," Patrick said.

"Fine - but you're going on Wednesday."

And for the first time in several days, Patrick smiled.

CHAPTER 12
Sunday, August 22, 1909

At eight o'clock Sunday morning, Leontine and Patrick showed up at the Tally Ho to take possession of the single-horse carriage she had arranged for the evening before. Given the time away and distance they would travel, she wanted to be sure to secure her favorite white Quarter Horse mare, Lindy Sue, and one of the carriages that included an overhead top. The Ortega family adobe home at Arroyo Hondo was almost thirty miles up the coast, just over a mile beyond the Barón rancho at Arroyo Quemada.

The day would be warm and the trip likely to last seven hours or more, depending on the number of stops they made along the way. They would not arrive at the Barón rancho until late afternoon, and then not have much time with Juan Carlos and his mother if they were to share the evening meal with her grand-uncle Hermogenes' family and settle in there for the night. It would be quicker if they traveled on horseback, but Patrick was not yet a skilled enough rider. Leontine also correctly assumed that Tesla would be joining them. Though he would spend much of the journey exploring on his own, he would need to recuperate on the carriage seat between excursions.

Leontine was dressed in her tan traveling suit, made from the sturdiest of cotton fabrics. The long overcoat extended past her knees so that the insidious road grime might have a more difficult time of finding its way beneath layers of clothing. The matching broad-brimmed hat had insertion points at the sides, through which she laced a sheer ribbon that she tied in a bow under her chin. She had cautioned Patrick to wear long pants for the journey as they would no doubt find it necessary to get out of the carriage at times when fording a wash or stream, or to help Lindy Sue maneuver through some sort of tangle or other. The scrub brush could be punishing and snakes were abundant.

She only had one suitcase, which barely managed to contain a simple cotton skirt, linen blouse, a night dress and a few toiletries. Patrick had his short pants and an extra shirt rolled up in a cylinder with his toothbrush tucked inside. Leontine slid it behind her suitcase and lashed it onto the luggage platform behind the cab. Then she tucked a wicker basket on the floorboard at Patrick's feet that contained a lunch of chicken sandwiches and fruit salad that they would enjoy somewhere along the line. The two canteens of water Uncle Remy had filled for them, and Patrick's camera, would easily fit on the seat between them.

For Patrick, this trip was to be a grand adventure. The furthest he had been from home in Santa Barbara was Mission Street, to visit the old mission overlooking the town. He looked forward to chronicling the route with his Kodak and had become adept at coming up with brief comments or useful descriptions he would inscribe in strips of red paper exposed between sections of film. This "autographic negative", hidden beneath a spring-loaded door and etched with a small stylus, would allow for the captions to appear along the edge of the photographed image. He had already prepared four pages in a new photograph album, having affixed gummed corners on the backing-stock to secure finished pictures in place.

For Leontine, it would be a journey through the past, her family history laying dense along the route they would travel. She set a brisk pace for Lindy Sue, traveling up De la Vina Street - which became Hollister Avenue once they crossed Mission Street – where the land opened up on the mountain side so that one could clearly see the old mission in the distance. To their left, Cottage Hospital was vaguely visible through a grove of walnut trees, the roof of the three-story building just cresting the top of the trees.

About an hour into their journey, they reached Cieneguitas, which Leontine said meant "little swamps" in the Chumash Indian language. Once they crossed over the wooden bridge at Cieneguitas creek, the old Catholic cemetery came into view, nearly covering the hill to their right. On the left was the Chapel of San Miguél, an adobe church that Leontine explained had been built for the Chumash Indian village that once surrounded it. "I remember they used have an old pump organ," she said.

"One day we'll come back and see if it's still in there."

Half an hour later, after passing several farms, Leontine and Patrick arrived in the small town of Goleta. The road was flanked by false-front wooden buildings that included William Warren's Meat Market, Dr. Rowan's office, Rafaela School, the Methodist church and an astonishing number of blacksmith shops to serve the farming community.

Farther still, they passed the impressive Sexton home, a magnificent two-story dwelling with a central third-story tower that included viewing windows in every direction. On the other side of Hollister Road was the Kellogg farm which Milo Potter leased to house the pigs, chickens, cows and squab that would land, deliciously transformed, onto Potter dining room plates every day of the week.

When they reached the old Birabent Hotel, Leontine stopped the carriage. She walked Lindy Sue over to a concrete watering trough at the side of the road while Patrick fetched his camera and one of the canteens from the carriage. Roadside businesses were paid a sum of three dollars per year if they would build troughs and keep them filled with fresh water for passing horses.

The two stood in the shade of the building sipping water as Leontine told Patrick a bit of her family's history. "My grandfather, Jean Marie Birabent, built this hotel in 1869. Back then it was the biggest building in the Goleta Valley. There used to be a store and saloon downstairs."

Patrick could see that rented rooms now filled the entire two-story structure, and that a single-story residence had been attached at one end. He looked around at the small farms and businesses surrounding the hotel and tried to imagine what it looked like fifty years earlier. How did people live back then? What did they do for fun? Patrick had no real experience of ancestry, and it seemed wondrous and mystical to him. "Was your grandfather born here?" he asked.

"Oh, no. He was from France. He came here when he was 19 with his best friend. It took them seven months to cross the Atlantic and sail all the way around South America to San Francisco.

Patrick envisioned the globe sitting on his work table back at the adobe. He was aware explorers and navy ships had traveled the route Lulu described, but for some reason this personal account made the journey seem more vast and daring.

"Why did they want to go to San Francsico?"

"My grandfather's brother moved there during the gold rush. Grandfather and his friend worked for him in the cattle trade. Sometimes they drove cattle down here and grandfather ended up marrying one of the Ortega girls. At one time, the Ortega family owned most of the land along the coast that you will see today."

Patrick traipsed around the building some more, then carried his camera out nearer the road again so he could fit the whole structure in one photo. Once done, he spotted something on the ground near the watering trough and bent to pick up what turned out to be just an old metal button, half-buried in the dirt. It was filthy and worn, but he could still make out the imprint of an eagle perched atop a sideways anchor. He didn't know if the button really was old, but it seemed old, perhaps because of all Lulu's talk of the past. He slipped it into his pocket for closer inspection later, thinking he might be able to figure out if it was from a uniform or something. He was overcome with a desire to peek in the windows of the old hotel and scrounge around the grounds for any other artifacts that might warrant research and investigation. He told Leontine he would love to have more time to poke around.

"We'll come back one day. There's more to come."

Two-and-a-half hours into their journey, they passed by the impressive entrance gate to the Glen Annie ranch, built by Colonel William Hollister, and named for his wife, Annie. The very road they were traveling was named for Col. Hollister, primarily because it led directly to his house – and because he paid for a substantial portion of its construction with his own funds.

"He built the Arlington Hotel," Leontine said, her voiced tinged with sadness. It had been just over a week ago, on Wednesday the fifteenth of August, that the Arlington Hotel burned down. The local citizenry had gathered in sorrow to watch the demise of what was once the most glorious structure in Santa Barbara. The loss seemed more personal somehow as they passed the broad wood-framed archway that led to Mr. Hollister's former home.

They continued along the Camino Reál, and in just over an hour Leontine pointed to the tower of a small stone church on top of a hill. A small cluster of buildings was situated near a creek a short distance beyond it. "It's the Naples church. We'll stop there for lunch."

As they neared the tiny community, Leontine turned off of the Camino Reál onto Langtree Avenue, explaining to Patrick that the street was named for a famous actress, Lilly Langtree. It was rumored that she had purchased an entire city block in the town, but whether or not the rumor was true, she never did arrive.

Leontine guided the carriage to the top of the hill and stopped in the shade of the church where they were able to take advantage of a gentle breeze blowing in from the ocean. They sat in the carriage eating their lunch of chicken and watercress sandwiches and a fruit salad of oranges, bananas, candied cherries and walnuts, as Leontine told Patrick a bit of the history of the place.

In the late eighteen-eighties John Williams, a successful lumber agent from St. Louis, and his wife Alice, spotted the location from a steamer ship on their way to San Francisco. They marveled at how closely it resembled the landscape surrounding Naples, Italy. Ultimately, they were able to purchase the land, and for nearly a decade the couple worked tirelessly to create a rural haven for vacationers and any persons interested in a pastoral life of retreat. They were certain that once the Southern Pacific Railroad was extended through the town their community would thrive. Sadly, Mr. Williams passed away before the railroad arrived and the dream never came to fruition. Alice had the church built so he could be buried in the place he loved most.

"It's Sunday," Patrick said. "How come there's no one here?"

Leontine drew his attention to the likenesses of two pug dogs carved in stone and mounted above the main entrance. "Alice loved her dogs so much she buried them inside with her husband. The people in town say they don't want to worship in a pet cemetery."

Once the eating was done, Patrick and Tesla circled the church to find the best photographic vantage point. He carefully composed the image in the viewfinder and got several shots of the structure and the tiny community along the creek at the bottom of the slope. He had hoped for a look inside as well, but it was locked up tight.

Next, they headed for the cluster of buildings alongside Dos Pueblos creek where Lindy Sue would be able to drink her fill and they could all cool off near the water. As they clopped through the center of town,

Patrick eyed the small businesses: a post office, blacksmith shop, Wells Fargo stagecoach office and the diminutive Naples Hotel. Leontine stopped the carriage in front of one large building so Patrick could get a shot of the town from the other side. When he climbed back into the carriage he noticed Leontine seemed sad when she looked at the building.

"What is this place?" he asked.

"The dance hall. They used to have hay rides to bring kids out here from town for dances. Ranch kids, too."

"Fun."

"It was fun. The very first time I came I met Vincent."

Leontine allowed herself another moment of wistfulness, then grabbed the reins and coaxed Lindy Sue toward the creek. While she had her drink of water, Leontine told Patrick that the area, Dos Pueblos, was named hundreds of years earlier for two Chumash villages that were once situated on each side of the creek, and that it had kept its name longer than any place she knew of. Then it was time to get back on the road.

By the end of another hour, the two had traveled some twenty miles from home and were approaching El Capitán. Leontine had many stories of this area as her family was integral in its evolution. She told Patrick how her great-great-great-great-grandfather, Jose Francsico Ortega, first arrived in 1769 as a scout for the very first land party to explore California, how he had discovered San Francisco Bay, and was the first comandante of the Santa Barbara presidio. She talked of how he had received the surrounding land as a grant when he retired from the army, and that it had belonged to her family for over one hundred years.

Less than three miles farther on, they passed Refugio Canyon. Here, Leontine relayed a story from 1818 when Spain was at war with Argentina. A man named Bouchard was hired by the Argentine government to attack Spanish possessions. At that time California was under Spanish rule and so became a target. Bouchard attacked and pillaged the state capital at Monterey, then sailed down the coast and stopped at Nuestra Señora del Refugio, the Ortega family's prosperous rancho, known to trading ships as a welcome port where they could sell their wares illegally. The Ortega family packed all of their treasures and fled up the Refugio Pass to the safety of Mission Santa Ines to escape the pirate Bouchard.

"The old Spanish chests in my living room are the very ones the family took with them when they ran."

It was early afternoon, nearly seven hours since leaving Santa Barbara, when the Barón orchards and adobe house at Arroyo Quemada came into view. As they neared the dwelling, they could see Juan Carlos waiting by a rail fence that surrounded the home, no doubt having observed their approach for some time. Leontine registered an air of deterioration around the farm without naming to herself what, specifically, created that impression. As Lindy Sue came to rest near the open gate, Juan Carlos hurried to help Leontine from the carriage. Tesla leapt from the seat and followed his nose along a path that wrapped around the house to the barn in back. Patrick jumped down as well and stood shyly investigating his shoes until Leontine could introduce him.

Leontine greeted Juan Carlos fondly and raised an arm so that he could slide into her embrace as she half-turned to present her young friend. When she looked into Carlito's eyes, however, she turned to him more fully. She could see that he was overcome, tears filling his eyes and in danger of spilling. He said, "You're here – " and then his voice cracked and they did spill. He swiped at wet cheeks impatiently and tried to regain his composure. Leontine drew him close and though he was now taller than she was, he buried his face in her neck and, just for a moment, let the tears flow, then pulled himself away and dried them with his shirt tail.

"What has happened?" Leontine asked. She saw his eyes flick in the direction of Patrick. "Patrick, this is Vincent's brother, Juan Carlos," she said over her shoulder. "Can you unhitch the carriage, please?" Patrick muttered a "hello" and Juan Carlos did the same, then Patrick busied himself with the task as Leontine and Juan Carlos moved a few steps away.

"What has happened?" Leontine repeated.

"I don't know what to do. I sent word for Tina and Gloria both, but Gloria just had a baby and Tina can't come until later this week." His sisters both lived in Santa Maria with husbands and families of their own.

"Is your mother okay?"

"I don't know. I don't think so. She won't…" His voice trailed off and he just shook his head.

"Why don't you help Patrick with the mare," Leontine said. Though

Juan Carlos appeared uncertain, her expression communicated that everything would be fine.

As the boys disappeared around the house with Lindy Sue, Leontine walked up the dirt path to the front door. She noticed that a section of fencing on one side of the dwelling had been pushed over by an aggressive succulent advancing into the yard. Portions of the fence rail were broken or missing, and the bright whitewash of paint had not been maintained. She halted in her advance to fully absorb the condition of the house. Peeling paint, dust and grass collecting on the porch, and dirt-caked windows, streaked from rains that had not been seen since early spring, combined to create an air of fatigue and abandonment. Something was dreadfully wrong. She stepped onto the porch and tapped on the door, lowering her head to listen intently for any signs of movement inside. There were none. After several moments, she tapped again more forcefully. Without waiting for a response, she tentatively opened the door and stepped inside.

The interior reflected the same bleakness as the yard, and though it was warm outside the place felt dank and chilly. Leontine removed her hat and gloves, then took a moment to open some curtains. Ashes from the fireplace had blown into the living room at some point and settled thickly on the cushioned furniture and wool rug. A plank table in the dining room looked eerie, a vase of dead flowers resting on an ash-laden tablecloth and flanked by grimy ceramic candlesticks.

Leontine called to Innocencia with a lightness of tone she did not feel. Silence. She poked her head into the kitchen and looked through the window to the back of the dwelling where she saw the expanse of the orchard and the barn where the boys were caring for Lindy Sue. Then she headed down a broad hallway that lead to the bedrooms.

Innocencia Cordero married Vincent's father, Rigoberto Barón, in 1879 when she was sixteen and he forty-eight. They had four children, Vincent the third in line, and worked the farm together until Rigo's death in 1900 at the age of sixty-nine. Leontine had found it challenging to connect with her nervous and tightly wired future mother-in-law. Small, fidgety and silent, she often covered her mouth with her hand, toying with her lips or gripping her own chin, as if to be certain nothing would escape. She was now forty-four, and though it had been just three years since Leontine had seen her, it was alarming how much she had aged.

Innocencia lay in her bed staring fixedly through her bedroom window. She did not turn her head to see who entered. Leontine tried not to react to unpleasant smells and approached the bed with forced composure, her voice calm.

"Innocencia, it's Leontine. Do you know me?" The frail woman's eyes darted to Leontine's face, then quickly returned to the window.

"Yes," she said, almost too quietly to hear.

Leontine stepped closer and perched on the edge of the bed. "Do you feel sick?"

Innocencia turned her head at last and looked directly into Leontine's eyes.

"Is Carlito…?"

"He's outside. I'm going to talk to him for just a minute and then we'll have a warm bath. Would you like that?" Innocencia furrowed her brow, deeply considering the question, until her gaze drifted back to the window.

Leontine hurried to find Juan Carlos and Patrick. She asked Carlito to heat water on the kitchen stove and fill the tin tub in the bathing room next to the kitchen. She told the boys to get Juan Carlos' horse ready to ride, saying it would be faster if they shared a saddle. They were to ride to Arroyo Hondo and come back with a wagon, and to ask if a comfortable bed could be made for Innocencia, as she was not well. She would need looking after until Tina could come from Santa Maria. One could see the weight lift from Juan Carlos' shoulders.

Once the boys were off, Leontine completed the task of filling the bathing tub. Through the window she could see the privy some thirty yards from the back door. She imagined how difficult it would be for Innocencia to walk that far, and she suspected the feeble woman had stopped eating so she could avoid making the trek.

Leontine returned to Innocencia and, adopting the matter-of-fact demeanor of a hospital nurse, helped her from her bed, then quickly stripped the soiled linens. She supported the feather-like weight of Innocencia's body as they walked slowly to the bathing room. There, Leontine coaxed and soothed the older woman out of her soiled bedclothes. She placed them on the back porch with the linens to be cleaned later, found fresh bedding in a wardrobe closet and hurriedly made the bed while Innocencia sat motionless in the tub of warm water. Leontine returned to tenderly wash her brittle body and, cradling her head, applied Castille soap to her hair, massaging ever so gently. Then she dried her off, slipped a night dress over her head, and combed out her hair. All without either woman speaking a word.

Leontine got her patient situated back into bed, then disappeared into the kitchen to make them both some tea, though Innocencia allowed hers to grow cold without taking a single sip.

Leontine looked out the window trying to gauge by the light how much time had passed. She sighed, feeling she had done all she could for the moment, then sat on the edge of the bed. Innocencia's hand rested next to her own body and Leontine slid her hand almost imperceptibly toward it. Innocencia drew hers back in equal measure.

"Inocencia, Hermogenes' boys are coming to get you. You're going to stay with them until Tina comes to bring you back home. Do you understand?"

Innocencia looked anxiously into Leontine's eyes and said, "Please, take Carlito with you."

"I can, of course, but surely he'll want to be with you."

"Please. Take him."

"All right," Leontine agreed, though internally she reserved the right to change the answer as the situation became more clear.

"I did something bad," Innocencia whispered.

"Do you want to tell me?"

Innocencia nodded. Leontine carried a chair to her bedside from its place near the window. Once seated, she leaned forward and gently took the older woman's hand after all.

"Tell me," she said.

CHAPTER 13
Gaviota – 1848

Rigoberto Barón rode silently beside Honorato Ortega, uncle to his young bride, Luz Maria Ortega Barón, now departed. The older man was quiet also, as yet unable to give voice to the ache in his chest and the catch in his throat. It was pointless to hurry. The men could provide nothing at the moment for the infant son left behind. Rigo's thoughts swirled inside him, images flashing - a night of daring with Luz Maria in Honorato's own orchard, the wedding soon after, hurried, yet joyous nonetheless, and his own face in mounting frustration and fear, as time revealed the enormity of his new responsibility. Pictures that led here, to this moment of loss and dread.

Rigoberto was the third son of Don Augustín Manuél Barón, who ran sheep and cattle on five hundred acres of the Ortega rancho. Don Augustín leased the land, but worked single-mindedly toward a goal of one day owning it for himself.

Rigo was just seventeen when his adulthood commenced so abruptly, and he had yet to declare a direction in life. With need of income instantly upon him, he grasped the first opportunity presented for employment: to work as a vaquero at Rancho Nojoqui. The rancho, located north of the Santa Ynez Mountain Range just beyond the Ortega's Rancho Refugio, was owned by Honorato's relative. No doubt it was this familial relationship that contributed to the offer of employment in the first place.

Rigo had been careful to disguise his lack of disappointment that Rancho Nojoqui was too far away to travel on a daily basis. With the arrival of the child fast approaching, it was widely agreed that Luz Maria would be better off in the care of her Tía Alma, rather than relocating to the rancho where she would be surrounded only by the vaqueros.

Honorato had awakened early in order to meet up with his nephew-in-law, deliver the heavy news and accompany him on the journey home. It would not do for the boy to travel alone and unsupported, given the bleak circumstances that awaited him. He came upon Rigo near a grove of alisals at the southern end of the ranch. Rather than backtrack to the Refugio Pass, they decided to take an old Indian trail that led through the Santa Ynez range, into the Arroyo Hondo and to the Camino Reál.

The two rode on in silence, anxiety twisting in Rigo's gut. Would he stay at Rancho Nojoqui now? Luz Maria's death had severed his immediate tie to the Ortega family, though thankfully, not that of his son, Juan Pablo. She had wanted the name and so the child would have it.

Where had the feeling gone? Where was the pride and anticipation leading up to the birth of Juan Pablo Barón? He felt nothing for the child now but resentment, and the weight of the burden of his very existence. Tears burned behind his troubled eyes, the more heated by shame that they were more for himself than for the girl who had lost her life bringing his son into the world. He glanced at Honorato, worried that the grieving uncle would see and understand his internal disgrace, but the man looked only at his own saddle.

As they descended into the Arroyo Hondo, Rigo noticed a thread of smoke coming from the far edge of the meadow below, a full half-mile from where the Camino Reál crossed the Arroyo Hondo creek. The smoke was just close enough to be seen before it spread into the ceaseless wind that rushed toward the cliffs above the shore. A campfire. What else could it be?

"Travelers," he told Honorato. "We should stop."

"Why?"

"I want…" but there was no reason, really. It was as cold as it ever got on the central coast of California two weeks before Christmas, although to most people in the country, it would hardly seem cold at all. They had been riding for hours, but neither were strangers to entire days in the saddle. In truth, Rigo wanted only to give himself a little more time to envision some way to behave like a man when he arrived at the rancho, a widower and father.

Honorato sighed and shaded his eyes as they reached the top of the meadow. Weary and sad, he had no heart for disagreement, so he reined his horse in the direction of the smoke.

As the two approached, they spotted five men waiting and watching, unwelcoming in their bearing and stance. Rigo's mount slowed of its own accord, and Honorato maneuvered his mare so that he rode in-between his young nephew-in-law and the stern contingent before them. The men had built their fire in a shallow arroyo off the lower edge of the meadow, though it provided little protection from the relentless wind. Six horses, focused only on the grass at their feet, stood hobbled some twenty yards further up the arroyo, along with two pack mules, absent their cargoes. Rigo counted the horses again, then glanced around for a sixth rider. Four of the men wore military jackets, ragged and filthy and not of identical issue.

Rigo and Honorato stopped fifty yards from the men. The one who spoke was forced to shout, his accent thick and Irish.

"Whaddayou want?"

Honorato said, "Nothing. A break. News."

News traveled faster than one might imagine along the increasingly occupied roads of California. Those who crisscrossed the length or breadth of the western territory traded warnings, stories and advice with fellow travelers as they wandered. Still, news had not traveled fast enough for the matter at hand. These men left behind them murderous crimes, heinous and brutal and so recently committed, they were still ahead of reports. The five sized up Honorato, dismissing young Rigo entirely, and apparently decided no threat was posed. They relaxed a small amount, offering nothing.

It was then that Rigo saw the sixth man. A beaten and bloodied body lay awkwardly on the ground beneath a gnarled pepper tree near the horses, hands lashed at his back. The man was obscured by a clump of thick chaparral and partially covered with a blood-soaked serape, the long black braid at his back exposing him as Indian. He looked like he might be dead. Rigo forced his eyes away, certain nothing good would come of reacting to the sight. He wondered if Honorato saw him.

"We've heard nuthin' of interest," said the Irishman.

Honorato sat motionless a moment, then nodded to the men and turned his horse. He kept is eyes straight ahead as his horse walked past Rigo, and so the boy suspected he had also seen the fallen man. He turned his own mount without looking at the men, then fell into step behind Honorato. The two did not speak until they were out of sight of the intimidating bunch.

"Was he dead?" Rigo asked when he felt safe enough to speak.

"I don't think so."

"What should we do?"

"Nothing," Honorato replied, but he did not move on. He looked up and down the Camino Reál that lead to the relative safety of his rancho.

"I know who he is," Rigo said. "I know his serape. He's called Juan the Indian."

Honorato stared over the ocean.

"We have to go back," Rigo said, but Honorato would have none of it.

"Then we would be more dead than Juan," he replied, and turned his horse toward Santa Barbara. Rigo did not follow. Which was the more terrifying he could not decide, the dying Indian and menacing clan, or the motherless child that bore his name awaiting his arrival at the rancho.

Rigo nudged his horse, a chestnut Morgan with jet-black mane and tail, to catch up to Honorato who had continued to walk his dapple-gray Thoroughbred slowly on. He passed his uncle-in-law, then stopped to turn and face the man he owed so much to already.

He said, "I'm going back," and lifted his chin to meet opposition.

"There are too many."

But this time Rigo would have none of it. "I'm going back," he repeated, then guided his horse off the trail toward the foothills.

"I'll send help." Honorato was prepared to do many things in the name of the spirit of Luz Maria, but dying was not one of them. His face set in determination, he took off at a run.

Rigo guided the Morgan up an arroyo to the ridge, then rode north a short distance until he spotted the trail, the sound of the wind masking that of the Morgan's hooves. Leaving his mount near the top of the meadow, he continued on foot and cautiously approached the campsite. He smelled the doused campfire even before he saw it. Dropping to his hands and knees, he crawled along until he could see what was happening below.

The men were gone, no doubt certain that Rigo and Honorato would report their whereabouts at the first opportunity. They fled leaving Juan where he lay. Rigo waited a good long time, and listened harder than he ever had in his life, to be sure the Indian was unguarded. At last, the boy crept down to the unfortunate man and spoke reassuringly to him as he untied the binding ropes. He rolled him over and tried to help him sit up, but some ribs were broken and it was too painful. Rigo went back to his horse and led the Morgan down to the site. He removed the saddle, then brought it, along with water and his saddle blanket, to where the injured man lay flat on his back. He set the saddle on the ground and slid the Indian into a propped-up position against it as gently as he could, then did his best to give him a drink of water. Juan's face was badly beaten and he was missing some teeth. There was no way Rigo would ever be able to get him onto a horse, even if he had one. The outlaws had taken the sixth horse and the mules. He asked the Indian if he thought he would be able to hold on if Rigo got him on the Morgan behind him. Juan closed his eyes and shook his head once. Rigo watched him, expecting each breath to be his last. Several minutes passed, then Juan opened his eyes just a slit, and he motioned for Rigo to move closer.

"Murderers," he managed to say.

"Who did they kill?" Rigo asked, without surprise.

Juan closed his eyes again, summoning strength. As the sun crested the sky, he told Rigo the horrible tale of the preceding week.

It had been August of 1848 when the first east coast newspaper reported the news of James Marshall's discovery of gold in Coloma, California the preceding January. Though a groundswell of gold fever was immediate, it could take as long as eight months to travel from the Atlantic coast to the western territory. One option was to sail around the tip of Argentina, a journey of ten thousand miles. Another route, the shortest and most expensive, was to stop at the mouth of the Chagras River on the eastern coast of Panama, travel through sixty miles of jungle by canoe and pack mule to Panama City, and thence northward by ship - if passage could be secured. Finally, one could risk the overland trek across the United States, a most dangerous and arduous undertaking. The first adventurers to make their way to the American River, therefore, were already situated in the west, or, at the very least, were already on the way there for one reason or another.

The massive blood-letting to come was set in motion the preceding October, when Peter Raymond, a veteran of Col. John C. Fremont's California Battalion, murdered a shopkeeper in Coloma who refused to sell him some whiskey. He escaped from jail, fled the gold country and, along his escape route, met Joseph Lynch. Born in Germany, Lynch had come to California from New York in 1846 to fight in the Mexican-American War. He rose to the rank of corporal in Col. Jonathon Stevenson's New York Regiment. When the Company was discharged in Los Angeles in September of 1848, Lynch, like most of his comrades, headed for the gold fields. Upon meeting Raymond, the two quickly agreed that robbery and murder would no doubt be much lighter work than mining, and by day's end they had befriended two miners on the road, killed them, and appropriated thirty ounces of gold and two horses.

During this time, another veteran of the California conflict, the sloop-of-war USS Warren, was functioning as a naval supply ship operating out of Monterey. In early November she was anchored at Sausalito when five of her crew stole a launch and deserted the ship. At Mission Soledad in the Salinas valley, these five came upon Raymond and Lynch who were traversing the region in search of more victims. Two of the crewmen decided to split off and headed for the mines. The other three, Peter Quinn, Peter Remer and Mike Bamberry, fell in with the pair of murdering thieves. As they headed south along El Camino Reál, they crossed paths with Juan the Indian, on his way to Mission Soledad in search of work. Through threats, intimidation and sheer numbers, they pressed him into service as their reluctant guide.

On the afternoon of the fourth of December, the six of them reached Mission San Miguél, now a private residence owned by William Reed and his family. Reed, an Englishman by birth, had come to California in the 1830s. He married a local girl, Maria Avila, and moved into the former Mission in 1845. The following year, Reed and his business partner, Antonilo Rios, were able to purchase the Mission buildings and surrounding land from Governor Pio Pico for the sum of $300. Increasingly successful in both farming and ranching, Reed and Rios made a healthy profit in the fall of 1848 running sheep up to the mines, earning far more than the men panning for gold.

On this particular afternoon, Maria, already mother to a two-year-old son, was very close to delivering their second child. Her midwife, Josefa Olivera, along with her eighteen-year-old daughter and four-year-old grandson, was staying with the Reed family until the arrival of the baby. Mrs. Reed's brother, Jose Vallejo, was visiting as well, and engaged in lively conversation with Reed. A negro cook and an Indian servant, his five-year-old nephew in tow, were also there and at work in the kitchen when the criminals arrived with their unwilling guide.

Reed welcomed the travelers into his home and purchased the thirty ounces of gold that Raymond and Lynch had stolen, as minted coin was more easily spent than gold dust when on the road. The miscreants stayed the entire night, enjoying the hospitality of Reed and his family. Unfortunately, at some point during evening conversation, Reed revealed that he already had more gold than his son could lift from his business at the mines, making a joke that soon he would be considered more banker than rancher.

The outlaws left the following morning, but had not travelled far when they agreed it would be a good idea to return to the Mission and separate William Reed from his pile of gold. When they reappeared, they complained to Reed that it had become too cold and windy, and asked if they might stay another day or two to wait out the cold front.

Juan the Indian was desperate to escape the criminals. He volunteered to retrieve firewood, intending to flee once out of sight of his captors. He knew his worst fear was upon him when, without warning, the air filled with the unthinkable sound of the blood curdling screams of women and children. To his own horror and shame, he froze in his tracks and covered his ears with his hands. The screaming stopped, and precious minutes passed until he found his legs at last and ran to the rear of the buildings. Crouching below a recessed window, Juan could hear the sound of breaking glass and splintering furniture inside as the devils ransacked the rooms. He stayed out of sight beneath the window until he heard them move to another part of the living quarters.

Steeling himself, he rose up and glanced quickly into the room, then went immediately to his knees. As familiar as Juan was with the evil men can construct, nothing he had ever seen came close to the massacre he beheld inside. The savagery was unimaginable. The ravaged corpses of Reed, his pregnant wife, her mid-wife and the mid-wife's teenage daughter lay strewn about the room, slaughtered in a vicious attack that had been accomplished in minutes.

Juan listened intently. It sounded like the men had moved outside to the front courtyard. Maintaining his crouched position, he hurried to the kitchen door, some fifteen feet away. He tried his best to peer inside from the doorway but could see nothing, and so, finally crawled inside where he found the bloodied corpses of the negro cook, the Indian servant and the servant's five-year-old son. Juan picked up a knife that had fallen from the hand of the dead cook, then stood in the center of the kitchen, turning slowly to take in the horror around him. It was surreal and he questioned his own sanity, until the sound of the band of killers running back inside the building for another load of treasure jolted him back to reality. He fell to his hands and knees and crawled frantically toward a storage alcove attached to the kitchen. Rounding the doorframe, he came up short and found himself face-to-face with the mid-wife's four-year-old grandson. The child's eyes were wide and staring, and it was chillingly apparent that the boy's soul had fled. Juan heard the men coming in his direction. There was no door between the storage room and the kitchen, and so no way to avoid detection. Juan had only seconds to act. As he envisioned the horrifying death of the servant's boy, and understanding what the murderers were capable of, he pulled the child toward him, gently covering his eyes with his hand and sheltering him with his own body. He laid his cheek on top of the boy's head and, whispering words of comfort, slit his throat with the cooking knife, holding him close while his life drained away.

When Quin and Remer appeared in the kitchen, covered in blood, their eyes wild and demented, they saw Juan immediately. The Indian did not move, grateful that he would soon join the child in his arms in the great beyond. The blood lust had run its course, however, replaced by the lust for riches. The Irishmen jerked Juan to his feet, kicking aside the body of the little boy.

They forced Juan to help as they piled all they could onto two of Reed's pack mules. Leather pouches of coin and bouillon, silver urns, pitchers and candlesticks, and odd items grabbed in haste – a branding iron, a hand-bellows and a wooden stool. When they had heaped the plunder onto the backs of the mules, they attached the animals' reins to the saddle horn of an Appaloosa and then forced Juan onto the horse to take charge of the safety of the bounty that had cost so many lives. It was not the threat of deadly violence that pressed Juan into service. It was his hope that he could somehow bring the devils down now that his own death was inevitable and welcome.

The outlaws headed for Mexico and spoke endlessly of the lives of comfort and leisure they would enjoy there, once arrived. As the troupe advanced south Juan watched for any opportunity to escape, or at the very least, thwart the gang's advance. He had no way of knowing how long it might take for someone to discover the horrendous scene at the Mission San Miguél.

In fact, the massacre was not discovered until the following day, by the unfortunate Don Francisco Branch and his brother-in-law, Don Juan Miguél Price. In passing by the Mission, they could not help but notice how quiet it was. Upon investigation and witnessing the horror inside, they raised an alarm, but so many men from the immediate area were gone to the mines it left few behind to guard the homes and families of those that remained. Several witnesses recalled seeing the men, including one from Rancho Atascadero who had delivered the mid-wife to Señora Reed. A description and warnings were carried by riders to ranchos all along the Camino Reál to the south.

When the outlaws stopped in the arroyo to cook and eat a calf they shot at the Rancho Alamos, they discovered Juan had disappeared as they were occupied gutting the animal and preparing the meat for the fire. Although they found him hiding in the sparse brush in fairly short order, they were furious at the time lost searching for him. They beat Juan savagely for the trouble he had caused, and no doubt would have ended his life in their rage, had they not been interrupted by the sighting of Rigo and Honorato.

Lynch suggested they bury the loot where they stood so they could ride more swiftly. They could split up, each taking a bit of the gold, then return to collect the rest of the bounty once the search for them had cooled down. Each swore an oath that they would band with the others and end the life of any one of them that tried to wait behind and steal off with the remaining treasure. They had only just finished burying the stolen goods when Rigo and Honorato showed up, and as soon as the two moved on, the killers rode off themselves.

It was simple enough for Rigo to find the pile of hastily gathered branches and leaves that covered the freshly dug earth where the riches were buried. Clearing the brush and digging with a flattened stone, Rigo soon held in his own hands the evidence that the horrid tale told by Juan the Indian was true.

Remembering the suffering man, Rigo returned to check on his condition, and found that Juan had passed. He laid the Indian flat, gathered his own saddle and blanket, and got the Morgan ready to ride. But ride where? And what would he do with the accursed treasure? It was far more than he could carry by himself. By the time he found anyone to help him, the murderers would no doubt have returned to take it back. He stood by the pit and stared at the fortune at his feet. He could dig another hole, it would not even need to be very far away, and re-bury the treasure where the villains would not know to look. He could come back with Honorato when the danger had passed. He would take a small part for himself and leave his uncle-in-law with the rest, as payment for taking over the responsibility of Juan Pablo. He would be free. Or, he could take what he could carry now and head for Monterey or San Francisco, returning to collect the rest of the stash once he was situated somewhere. He could leave Honorato out of it – and Juan Pablo forever unknown.

He at least became clear that whatever plan he ultimately enacted, they all began with him transferring the loot to another location, and he was betting he had little time to accomplish it. At the foot of an ancient pepper tree, he cleared dead leaves and branches and dug several pits, filling each with a portion of the treasure. He took great care to do a better job of disguising the hiding place than the murdering thieves had done, and, when he was done, he dragged Juan's body to the original pit and rolled him into his grave for the murderers to find on their return. He folded Juan's arms across his chest, then slid a silver cross beneath one hand. Hopefully, God would see the symbol and understand that Juan had tried to do right.

By December tenth, the news of the massacre had reached Santa Barbara, and a party of fifteen Barbareños, headed by Don Cesário

Lataillade, went to the Chumash rancheria at Cieneguitas in hopes of catching the outlaws as they passed through, but they were too late. The following morning, however, they learned that five men fitting the description of the murderers had been spotted when they stopped for supplies, and Lataillade and his men caught up with them on the crest of the second barranca overlooking the ocean at Ortega Ridge, just south of Santa Barbara. A gun battle ensued with many shots fired by all concerned, but Don Cesário was holding the posse at such a distance, none of the bullets found their mark. But the five were cornered, and Lataillade reasoned that time, gunpowder and ammunition were on their side.

But alas, one member of the posse, Ramón Rodriguez, grew tired of waiting. He mounted his horse and ran straight for the murderers, guns blazing. He wounded Bamberry who fell to the ground. As he continued his rampage, Rodriguez brought himself directly into the sight line of the fallen man's weapon. Bamberry fired into him and Rodriguez fell to the ground, dead. The rest of the killers ran toward the beach. Peter Raymond, trailing much blood, headed into the ocean, but the effort was too much, and he soon slipped beneath the waves. The remaining three were captured without further incident, bound and gagged and taken back to Santa Barbara for trial.

On Wednesday, the thirteenth of December, a committee comprised of three men; Thomas Robbins, Luís Burton and Enriqué Carnes, was elected to hear testimony from the surviving marauders. Quin, Remer and Lynch placed much of the blame on the two who had been killed, and all named Juan the Indian as the mastermind and worst offender. Nevertheless, on Christmas Eve, a jury elected by the citizens of Santa Barbara gathered to examine the evidence and testimonies and decide the fate of the criminals. In the end, the men confessed their sins, and after receiving the Last Sacraments from Father Rubio, they were lined up against an adobe wall in the heart of town and executed by firing squad for their crimes.

Four months after the massacre at the Mission San Miguél, Don Lataillade was cleaning a shotgun taken from one of the killers in the stand-off at Ortega Ridge. The nipple appeared plugged with shot, so he removed the barrel and put one end into the fire. The load was still in the

gun, and it fired its last shot into the side of Don Cesário. He lived for
a few hours more, then succumbed to his wounds, the twelfth and final
victim of the Mission San Miguél murderers.

These events would remain unknown to Rigo for a very long while.
He made the decision to take some of the coins and ride north to San
Francisco, with a plan to return for the rest of the treasure as soon as
possible. Only days after his arrival in the chaotic city, swollen to the
point of bursting with the daily arrival of desperate men in search of gold,
Rigo was robbed on the street. The men who attacked him immediately
fought between themselves. One shot the other and ran away with the
money. A witness came forward, saying it was Rigo who killed the man -
for what gain, Rigo never knew.

The boy was quickly tried and found guilty of murder. Because he
was so young, and his victim an assumed criminal himself, he received
a sentence of only five years. But jail is a terrible place, and Rigo became
a killer in truth when one morning his cellmate was found dead on
the floor, strangled sometime during the night. Though the judge had
suspicions of why a young boy might have good reason to fight off his
cellmate with deadly force, murder is murder, and so he declared that
when the original sentence was served, Rigo was to be transferred to the
new state prison in San Quentin for an additional twenty years.

The end of his long imprisonment found Rigo's perspective on the
events of his life vastly changed. During the first decade of his captivity,
rage, self-pity, desperation and fear chipped away at his soul until it
all but disappeared. Then, in his eleventh year, he befriended a cleric
who visited the prison regularly in an effort to reclaim errant souls for
the Lord. Through the ensuing years, query and conversation with this
gentleman ultimately gave rise to a more expansive and forgiving heart,
and thankfully, the middle-aged man who emerged from San Quentin in
the winter of 1873, headed back to Santa Barbara filled with purpose and
gratitude for his life. He would atone for past sins and devote what years
he had left to selfless endeavors that might bring peace to other hearts.
Life offers no guarantee, however, that satisfactory outcome will follow
earnest action, no matter how wholesome the intent.

When Rigo met his son at last, it was to finally understand the consequence of the choice he made the day he left for San Francisco. Juan Pablo, now a man of twenty-six years, had grown into a drunkard and a brute. He earned his living as a ruffian, hired by men more timid or slight to influence the actions of other men, through intimidation and physical harm. Any money he earned was quickly spent on drink, gambling and whores. He seemed destined for an early grave. It was somewhat surprising he had not found one already.

When Rigo first approached his son, who was cheating at cards in the back room of a makeshift brothel and saloon on Ortega Street, Juan Pablo simply stared at the man before him, unable to take in the information that this was his father. He ordered Rigo to put up some money and get in the game or go away. But the father persisted, imploring to be heard, offering heart-felt apology and promises of love and support.

The love of a father was something that held no allure for Juan Pablo, but a promise of support, however undefined, was something he felt worth exploring. Rigo moved Juan Pablo into the small house he was renting on Salinas Street, and for six years did his best to alter the trajectory of the life he had set into motion so long ago.

When Rigo had first moved into the house, many months passed before he made his way to the site of the cursed treasure. Convinced of its evil, he initially attempted to force the thought of it from his mind, or persuade himself it must have been found and made off with by now. Having spent all of his adult life in prison, however, he was finding it difficult to make his way. The fortune called to him, ever louder in his mind. And then the day came when he sought it out, finding the resting places easily and seeing they were undisturbed. And then the day he brought a shovel - only to confirm with his own eyes what he already knew was true, the riches were there, waiting. And then the day he took some of it away – just enough to purchase the very farm where Honorato and Alma had tried to help him so long ago, with a solemn vow to leave the rest. But the orchard did not thrive, and his farmhouse was soon overrun by his violent son and his heartless companions. All of it was cursed, as he knew it would always be, and Rigo understood that his cause was lost.

Innocencia came to his door one day to plead on behalf of her father.

Juan Pablo had been hired to settle a debt that, if collected, would leave her homeless, penniless and alone. Though Rigo did his best to intercede, Guillermo Cordero was beaten and banished, his worldly belongings transferred to the debtor and Juan Pablo's contract fulfilled. Out of guilt and atonement, Rigo offered Innocencia shelter. She quietly went about setting the farmhouse to rights, and it was not long before gratitude and appreciation for her work turned into something more. Innocencia was deathly afraid of Juan Pablo, however, and his unsavory associates as well. In his heart Rigo abandoned his derelict son once again, and he proposed to Innocencia. She agreed to marry on one condition - that Juan Pablo and his frightening companions be sent away - forever. Though Rigo promised her it would be done, she did not believe.

It was then that Rigo told his soon-to-be wife the entire story of the Mission San Miguél massacre, the cursed treasure and the toll all of it had taken on his life thus far. He called his son ruined, recognizing Juan Pablo to be as cursed as the treasure itself. It could do no more harm, he reasoned, to give over just enough of the money to provide Juan Pablo with a place of his own in Santa Barbara - assuming that once he had no use for Rigo's support, he would keep his distance. Innocencia begged Rigo to give all of the money to Juan Pablo. If it was as cursed as it seemed, why keep any at all? But there she had overstepped. Rigo assured her he would do what was right, that she could trust him, and that there would be no more discussion about it. That very night, when Juan Pablo headed into town for another night of depravity, Rigo took a lantern and a shovel and told Innocencia he would be back soon. Minutes later, she followed behind him, quiet, careful and cloaked in darkness.

Innocencia fell silent then, and Leontine found herself uncertain if the story was finished. It was much to take in, and at the moment, she needed to get the older woman situated for travel. Leontine let go of Innocencia's hand and rose from her chair. She leaned over her patient and brushed her hair from her face.

"We need to get ready. Carlito will be back any minute."

"You have to take him with you," Innocencia implored. "It's a son for a son, don't you see?" Innocencia said. "Or a hundred sons. Who knows what he's done?"

"I don't understand."

"Rigo thought Juan Pablo found the treasure on his own, but it was me. I told him where it was. The ones who died after...it was because of me." Innocencia covered her mouth with her hand and closed her eyes against escaping tears.

Leontine checked the light through the window again. Dusk was upon them, and she knew the boys would arrive soon. No doubt there was more to the story, and Leontine was keen to hear it, but it would have to wait.

plaza and boathouse

Los Banos pool

Castle Rock

Potter Hotel

367

The Potter Country Club
Visitor's Card
The privileges of the Club House
are hereby extended to

Mr. Francis S. Fordyce

for two weeks from date

Secretary

• SANTA BARBARA, CALIFORNIA •

Request of   M. M. Potter

Date August 19th, 1909

PLEASE PRESENT THIS CARD EACH TIME AT CLUB HOUSE. WHEN SIGNING CHECKS
FOR CAFE, BUFFET, AND GOLF LINKS, USE THIS CARD NUMBER SIDE OF SIGNATURE.

Potter Country Club, Santa Barbara, Cal.

Potter Country Club

South End, Southern Pacific Depot, Santa Barbara, Cal.

Depot benches and Neal Hotel

Leadbetter Mansion

Mr. Birabent's Hotel

Col. Hollister's Ranch

Naples Church

Town of Naples

Mr. Ortega

Arroyo Hondo Adobe House

CHAPTER 14
Sunday, August 22, 1909

Daisy removed the single page of her account of the unfortunate incident at Castle Rock from the typewriter and rose to place it on O'Brien's desk. Though it was Sunday, she knew he would be in sometime in the afternoon to approve content and layout for all six pages of the *Daily Independent* for Stevie, the Sunday typesetter. Stevie would begin his work day at 6:00 p.m. so that Donald, the pressman, could begin his work by 5:00 a.m. in order to make the morning delivery. Monday editions tended to be a bit more sparse so that on Sunday most of the staff could have a moment to catch their breath.

The entire effort had proved vexing in the extreme. Daisy could have told the whole tale in one sentence: "A Los Angeles attorney turned up dead at Castle Rock, but no one knows why or how." Her wording felt forced and disjointed and she struggled with every sentence. She consciously fought the urge to leap from her chair and just keep digging until she uncovered the story that would burst onto the page without so much toil. Why broadcast wide-ranging ignorance to the general readership? Although, it should be acknowledged that anyone who had heard anything at all about the event would rush to the Monday morning edition to satisfy curiosity. Whatever her personal motivations, Daisy was chiefly employed to sell newspapers, and so she persisted. Once the task was complete she would direct her energies toward the ferreting of facts, and she had a good idea of where to begin.

A quarter of an hour later, with notebook and pen in hand, Daisy sought out her colleague, Owen Reed. She crossed State Street and cut through the narrow walkway between buildings to the Stafford Saloon just behind the Woodward & Thon barbershop. When she pushed through the door, she was immediately greeted by the penetrating aroma of bacon. An enormous tin plate of the tempting fare, soaking in a greasy pool of its own making, was laid out on the bar just inside the door, a technical adherence to local law requiring that liquor be served only in eating establishments on Sundays. Daisy was a huge fan of bacon and would normally have helped herself to a rasher or two, but decided against dealing with greasy fingers.

The small establishment fit only four tables in the sawdust-covered floor area, with the entire space of the room dominated by the massive bar itself. Behind the bartender's area rose seven feet of heavily-festooned cupboards and shelving, displaying liquor bottles and drinking glasses to best possible advantage. The surrounding walls were decorated with Indian artifacts and stuffed animal heads, ranging in size from a giant elk to a diminutive jack rabbit – and everything in between. The long side of the bar was for standing, a brass rail installed to place one's foot upon while resting one or both elbows on the bar. The short side of the bar, facing the entrance door, had but two tall stools. Only one was normally available, however, as the other was perpetually occupied by Owen Reed.

Reed had an incredible tolerance for alcohol consumption, and though he downed impressive quantities of the substance every day, his mental capacities appeared eternally unchanged. Nonetheless, the lifestyle was apparent in his barroom pallor, bulging watery eyes, stick-thin malnourished limbs, and the expanding orb of his over-taxed liver.

Although Daisy appreciated the general ambience of the typical saloon as much as the next newspaperman, she had judged Reed harshly at first, chafing at his designation as "lead reporter" when all he did was nurse whiskies at the bar. It had not taken long for her to understand that news tended to seek out Owen Reed for the telling rather than the other way around. Daisy tossed her notebook on the bar, perched on the other stool and ordered a whiskey. She remembered in the moment that come October she would be forced to settle for ginger ale. Irksome.

At nearly sixty, Owen Reed was past caring about most aspects of life. From his point of view there was never anything new. No pronouncement he had not heard, no surprising character or unsuspected motivation. No mystery, no allure, no excitement. He waited out the sun in the dimness of the saloon, then waited out the darkness, sleepless and alone in his lamp-lit room above the Alexander & Redington real estate office a few doors down State Street.

He had been happy as a young man, with a wife and two sons. But in the winter of 1891, they were lost, one by one, done in by the Russian flu. His only solace was that his wife had died first, and so avoided the heartbreak of the death of her sons. His detachment and total lack of judgment – or interest for that matter – for any tale, made him a perfect receptacle into which others would pour rivers of information. Confession, obsession, manipulation, speculation – it was all the same to Owen Reed. He offered nothing but a public written report which seemed to bestow validation, or something like it, to the stories' tellers. And that, apparently, was enough.

Daisy and Reed shared an unspoken bond as reporters and their interactions were, without exception, occupational in nature. They eschewed the normal conventions of social interaction and invariably got right to the point.

"What's happening out there at the lake in Hope Ranch?" Daisy asked, without even the preamble of a greeting.

"A pet project of Ned Harriman's. He's president of the railroad."

Daisy's expression communicated she did not need to be told who Ned Harriman was.

"A trackless trolley – whatever good that will do us all," Reed said.

"You know anything about the guy in charge? Patillo?"

Reed gave a derisive snort. "Patillo's not in charge. He's just the poor sap hired to waste time and money."

"What would you say if I told you there is reason to believe Francis Fordyce died in Hope Ranch?"

Reed raised an eyebrow – an extreme reaction for him – and appeared to give the idea some thought. Daisy filled him in on the sketchy details known so far.

Reed replied, "There was a story on Patillo a couple of years ago if you can find it. He had an asphalt company in Carpinteria that went bust. We wrote about it. Might be something, I don't know. Tons on Harriman, of course."

Daisy's mouth became a line. Slogging through archived boxes of papers for tidbits of information was far from her favorite aspect of journalism. Nevertheless, it was a big part. She sighed, pushed her untouched drink over to Reed, and stood to return to the office.

"If Patillo's not in charge out there, who is?"

"Lovell, Harriman's right hand. But you'll never get an interview."
To which Daisy raised her eyebrow. How she did love a challenge.

Daisy returned to the office and grabbed the stack of most recent issues of the *Daily Independent* that had yet to be collected into bound volumes of archived editions. She glanced out the window for a last glimpse of the sun, then disappeared into the morgue. She was a couple of hours into her search, sitting Indian-style on the floor and surrounded by small pyramids of paper-board boxes crammed with photos and documents related to back issues of the newspaper. The boxes were chock-full but well-ordered, and she already had a tidy stack set aside in which a quick-skim reading had revealed something at least remotely related to the people and events at hand. She was leaning against the boxes scanning a story about the Pacific Improvement Company when, to her great surprise, she looked up to see Owen Reed leaning on the doorway, somehow untethered from his barstool.

"I don't know why I didn't want to tell you," Reed said, "but Patillo came to see me yesterday."

Daisy set her newspaper aside, looking up at Reed from her seated position on the floor. "Do tell," she replied.

"All he said was there's some shady business going on out at the project and he just wanted someone to know in advance that if anything bad ever happens out there, he's not involved."

"A dead body is bad."

"Agreed."

"Sure sounds like he's involved."

"I would say so. Thanks for saving me a trip to Hope Ranch," Reed said, and then left Daisy to her rummaging. She was tempted to stop what she was doing and find the quickest way out to the project site – no doubt the Potter motorbus – until she remembered it was Sunday.

In the end, her slogging proved more than fruitful. Not only did she find the article written about the demise of Patillo's company, Carpinteria Asphalt & Paving, but an associated box of documents as well that included a copy of the lawsuit between the City of Glendale and Patillo's company. The attorney of record was a name unknown to her, but the name of the firm he worked for glowed on the page as if lit by a beacon from heaven – Fordyce & Strawn.

Daisy took the steps back up to the office two at a time, eager to get going, and mentally ticking through a list of possible next courses of action. The second she entered the office, however, the balloon of excitement drifted into the atmosphere. Tom O'Brien was at his desk and he was talking to her brother. When Will responded to O'Brien's sighting of her and turned around, she was crushed to see the look on his face - fear. Without a thought in her head, Daisy set the papers on the nearest available surface, walked into her boss's office and buried her face in her brother's chest. She didn't see it, but the look of fear immediately vanished, replaced by a tear of relief. Tom O'Brien mumbled something about someplace else he needed to be and left the siblings alone in his office.

Daisy finally pulled away and looked up at her brother. He seemed so old. Like a man now. Then he reached up to swipe the tears from his cheek and she saw only the little brother she had cared for all his life.

Daisy asked the obvious first question, "How did you find me?"

"I saw your name in a newspaper from Santa Barbara."

Daisy nodded and walked around the desk to sit in O'Brien's chair. Will stood where he was, trying desperately to remember all the things he was intent on saying to his sister. She could feel it boiling within him as he looked at his shoes, and she sat back in the chair to brace for it.

"How could you do it?" Will finally asked, still looking at the ground, hands now clenched at his side.

Daisy did not respond until he looked up at her. "I just couldn't take it anymore."

"Violet's gone to Santa Rosa. She's getting married."

Now it was Daisy who lowered her eyes. Violet. Married.

"Dad took off with that other lady." Will glowered at his sister and shot information at her like bullets. "Ma took Junior to Octavia Street. She doesn't come around at all. If I show up at the docks, Dad gives me some money, but it's never enough. The landlord is fed up and if he kicks us out, then what? Rose is only eleven. She can't take care of Iris and Lilly by herself and I have to work. You have to come home, Daisy."

Daisy shifted her gaze out the window. The street was quiet. "I did it," she said. "And I was far from eleven years old."

"Rose isn't like you. She wants to spend more time at school."

What's wrong with me? Daisy wondered silently. She felt detached, as if he was describing some family she had never met. She should feel anger now, or indignation. At the very least guilt. She looked into her brother's face, recognizing the frustration and desperation he felt. But even that did not stir her. She felt nothing at all.

"Just come home, Daisy," Will repeated. "We need to get back."

Daisy sighed and stood up from the desk. She asked, "Where are you staying?"

"I slept in the train station last night."

"I'll get you a room downtown."

"Why? We're just….just come on," Will said, his frustration peaking.

"I'm not doing that, Will, so get a room and we'll talk about it later. Do you need money?"

"I'll be at the station," he said, and slammed out of the office.

Daisy was still sitting in O'Brien's chair when he returned and tentatively poked his head into the office. Daisy sighed and stood, but then sank right back down and covered her face with her hands.

"How'd that go?" O'Brien ventured.

Daisy spoke into her cupped hands saying, "Really great."

"I see that. Do you want to…?" But O'Brien was completely out of his depth.

"I think I'm a bad person," Daisy admitted, then she lowered her hands and stood to return the desk to her boss. O'Brien walked around her.

"That's one person's opinion," he said.

"Okay, what about you? Do you think I'm a bad person?"

Without meaning to, O'Brien paused and looked directly and deeply into Daisy Merrie's eyes. "Oh, no," he said quietly. For a long moment Daisy held his gaze, waiting for him to blink and prove himself insincere. But he didn't do it. He didn't blink. It was Daisy who finally looked away when she turned to leave the room.

"Thank you," she whispered before closing the door.

CHAPTER 15

Nicholas walked out of the McDermott Funeral Home on the corner of Haley and State Streets, where the body of Francis Fordyce was currently stowed, and paused to consider what he would do next. He had spent the preceding few hours with county coroner Antonio Ruiz and Dr. Simon Bauer, a pathologist from the east coast who was in town for the summer and staying at the Mascarel Hotel. Ruiz was not a physician, and though there were more than a dozen fine doctors and surgeons in the Santa Barbara area, none of them specialized in pathology. Dr. Bauer had seemingly had enough of his holiday and was eager to assist with the post-mortem and embalming of the deceased, and to offer his opinion regarding the cause of death of the Los Angeles lawyer.

The autopsy proved most productive and educational. Nicholas knew the man had not drowned because the lungs were free of water. He learned from Dr. Bauer that neither did he die from his broken neck, which also occurred post-mortem, but most likely by electrocution caused by something he had grabbed or held in his hands. When he more closely examined the charred flesh of Fordyce's hands, made all the more grisly because of the time in the water, Nicholas remembered that Patrick had seen them when he found the body. A wave of protectiveness washed through him, so intense it made him sick to his stomach. He was overcome with an urge to hold Patrick, and almost regretted for a moment allowing him to accompany Leontine on her excursion up the coast.

But now that the business of the post-mortem was over, and with Patrick away, Nicholas was free to do as he liked – a situation so rare he was at a bit of a loss in what to do. He did need another conversation with the inscrutable Mrs. Fordyce. They had spoken by telephone earlier in the day when she gave permission for the autopsy and to ready the body for transport to Los Angeles where her husband would ultimately be laid to rest. Nicholas was well aware that people process grief in their own way and in their own time, and that it is unwise to gauge overall character based on reaction to the trauma of injury, illness or death. Nevertheless, there was something disconcerting about how the young widow presented herself in the face of her personal tragedy. He had witnessed many times how grief could manifest as standoffishness, anger or a retreat into minutia – among countless other things. The young Widow Fordyce was proving difficult to assess, however. Her mannerisms and comments seemed appropriate enough, except that all were delivered as if for a staged play. She operated from a layer of remove that could be grief or a clear assessment of an overwhelming situation, but might just as easily be a serious depression or even dissociation. Whatever it was, it was not setting right in his mind and he wanted his next encounter with her to be face-to-face so he could evaluate if she needed help.

A trip to the Leadbetter mansion was definitely in order, and Nicholas headed down State Street toward the Boulevard on foot so he could think about the victim and his young widow as he walked. When he got to the train station just beyond Montecito Street, he found his thoughts usurped by another matter, that of Miss Pearl Chase and her scheduled departure by train the following morning. Nicholas sighed deeply, then crossed the street to the station and took a seat on an empty bench in the open receiving area.

As studiously as he tried to avoid the topic, it continued to present itself in his mind for resolution - something he was beginning to suspect might be hopeless. He felt positively infested with reasons why and why not to commit himself to Miss Chase's future, and so weary of the indecision it was all he could do to keep from surrendering altogether and simply entrust his fate to a flip of a coin.

In the eight years since Audrey passed, Nicholas had kept his eyes open for whatever situations appeared best for his son. Initially, he assumed a new mother would be best. But mother to Patrick would be wife to himself, and that was something he was not then ready to contemplate. His own parents were already deceased, killed in a fire at the iron foundry where they met and both worked. His brother's wife had stepped into the void, but with twin boys of her own, there was only so much she could do. Nicholas was ashamed to admit it, but Patrick had been so calm and bright and capable of entertaining himself that he left him on his own on many occasions – even as a very young child.

It was true his decision to pursue a career in medicine had completely absorbed any interest or energy Nicholas possessed outside of the care of his son for many years. In any case, there were few women around during medical school, and those in proximity tended to focus almost exclusively on their medical training. The added difficulty of pursuing a medical career while female would allow for nothing less. Once graduated, there came a year of hospital training, then the move to Santa Barbara and setting up of his private practice. At times he felt lonely for a mate, someone to share his days with – and his nights. Someone to laugh with who would delight in his extraordinary son and perhaps bring him another, or the gift of a little girl. He watched and waited for the dormant feelings of love and desire to rekindle and spark, coaxed back to life by the breath of some woman who could finally make him feel the way Audrey had. But now he doubted that would ever happen, and so wondered if he should just settle for something less, however unfair that might be for any would-be bride.

He realized now that inaction can itself be termed action at some point, and that his silence and passivity had created an expectation in Pearl that she might have a future with him to consider. However, it would mean a future as Patrick's mother as well, and his son's relationship with Leontine Birabent muddied the waters further. Nicholas was not exactly sure how he even felt about Leontine. Grateful, certainly, and increasingly dependent on her love for his son. There was no question that she provided the emotional support and stability of a mother, and seemed more than happy to do so. He would be lying to himself if he did not admit to imagining a life with her. He was comfortable in her presence, finding it most often a relief for his spirit. But whatever had happened with her fiancé seemed unresolved for her, and he was uncertain whether their shared histories of tragedy and love for dear Patrick could translate into a sustainable marriage. Their separate sorrows might consume them individually and keep them forever at arms' length with each other. And if he brought another woman into the fold, who among them could agree to Patrick's relationship with Leontine?

He was pretty sure the answer was 'none of them', and any idea of coming between Patrick and Leontine was unthinkable – at least for the foreseeable future.

Pearl had pressed the issue obliquely a few days earlier, so he knew the time was upon him to signal to her if he was considering her for a wife. She had graduated *suma cum laude* with a History of Letters degree from the University of California the preceding June, and in the course of several seemingly off-hand conversations, had gradually laid out her immanent life choices for Nicholas. She had been offered a position at the Bancroft Library at Berkeley which she felt well worth considering. After all, academic life offered enviable benefits of respect and social standing. On the other hand, Pearl felt increasingly perturbed at the way Santa Barbara was managing its operation and growth, and never seemed to tire of expressing passionate opinions about what should or should not be done about trash or trees or buildings or anything else for that matter. She told Nicholas she felt a responsibility, almost a calling, to roll up her sleeves and work toward creating in Santa Barbara an example of how an effective system of municipal governance, support and expansion could be implemented. She told him she just wasn't sure, and was waiting for some kind of sign to direct her final decision of whether to stay at Berkeley or go retrieve her belongings and return to Santa Barbara for good.

Nicholas turned his gaze to where the empty tracks curved and disappeared quickly from sight. He cleared his throat, squared his shoulders and stood up, and in that instant, released both himself and Miss Chase from his indecision. He would set her free.

Continuing his walk toward the Leadbetter estate, Nicholas felt a lightness in his step he now realized had been absent for some time. He smiled and tipped his hat to all who crossed his path. Grateful for the cooling marine layer that had yet to give in to the sun for the day, he covered the mile-long distance to his destination in no time at all.

As he approached the mansion, he saw Margaret Ramirez directing two young Mexican men as they loaded a carriage with several boxes and a large steamer trunk. She stood on the porch, issuing orders and pointing with one hand, the other wrapped around the drooling babe on her hip. Nicholas noticed a difference in the young woman. The trendy metropolitan look was gone, replaced by the simple cotton skirt and linen blouse most women in town tended to favor. He noticed also that she did not try to hide her irritation when she caught sight of the unexpected visitor.

"Hello," Nicholas said when he was within earshot. "Is Mrs. Fordyce at home?"

"Not at the moment," Margaret said.

"Do you expect her?"

"I do not."

Nicholas turned to observe the activity at the carriage. "Traveling?"

"What is it you want, Doctor? I can leave a message for her."

"I have the results of the post-mortem."

The edginess left Margarita's voice immediately. "You're welcome to wait," she said. "Do you mind if I ask the outcome?"

"I should share that with his wife first. You understand."

Margarita's gaze shifted from the loaded carriage to the doctor and back again. Clearly anxious to be done with the surprise visit and on her way, she said, "I don't know what to suggest."

Nicholas decided to look for Mrs. Fordyce later and said as much to Margarita. He tipped his hat and headed back down the drive. Halfway to the Boulevard he was passed by the over-loaded carriage. As he watched it advance toward the beachfront, it occurred to him that, to date, he had never actually seen Caroline Fordyce take physical possession of her own child. In every instance the baby was in the arms of Margarita Ramirez. He wasn't quite sure what to make of it, but noticed the thought furrowed his brow and cast yet another element of suspicion regarding the well-being of Caroline Fordyce. One would normally expect her to cling more tightly to that which remained of her union with her late husband, and yet, he had never witnessed a look or heard a word that she possessed any thoughts about her son at all. He stopped and turned to look at the mansion where she was living, and acknowledged that Francis Fordyce, III was actually far from the only thing left behind. He could only hope the boy was considered the most important.

By the time Nicholas reached the Boulevard his legs were tired and his feet were sore. He decided to stop at the foot of Castillo Street to catch the trolley back into town. He would stop at his office, though he couldn't think of anything pressing there that needed his attention, then head home. It was the first time Patrick had been away since their move to Santa Barbara and he missed his son terribly. How would he fill this yawning gap of time? He would deliver Miss Chase to the train station in the morning and express to her his support, should she decide to take the position at the Bancroft Library. Then, thankfully, the rest of his Monday would be a normal, busy work day. But first he would have to get through this very solitary Sunday night.

To his unending delight, when the trolley car appeared Nicholas saw Daisy rise from a seat inside and make her way toward the exit. He smiled broadly, waiting for her to see him. As he watched her advance, he realized that the girl was uncharacteristically downcast. She had not raised her eyes to take in her surroundings even once. He moved closer to the trolley car so she would be sure not to miss him. Not wanting to startle her, Nicholas spoke her name and touched her lightly on the arm when she stepped to the ground. When she looked up, he could see that she had been crying. His face immediately reflected his compassion and concern, and though surrounded by a dozen others mounting and dismounting from the trolley, Daisy began to bawl unabashedly. Nicholas offered a handkerchief, put an arm around her shoulders, then walked her to the nearest bench near the Plaza fountain to soothe her and find out what was wrong.

Once Daisy regained some composure, she explained that she was having some kind of delayed reaction to the unexpected arrival of her brother and the news he had disclosed about her family. She told Nicholas that Will was waiting for her at the train station, but that she was afraid to talk to him again. Afraid that the new life she had only just begun was already at an end. Afraid that she was selfish and even a little bit mean. She had climbed aboard the trolley intending to find him at the station and tell him to go back without her – but at the last moment she just couldn't do it, and stayed in her seat to the end of the line. She hated the thought of Will waiting for her, but also worried that in her current condition he would persuade her that he was right - her sisters needed her and it was her duty to return to San Francisco.

"I need time to think," Daisy said. "I offered to pay for a room for him so we could talk about it more tomorrow, but he won't wait."

Nicholas took in the story without comment. It had not occurred to him before this moment that Daisy must have had a life somewhere before the day she appeared at Leontine's door.

"We'll go together," he assured her, "and for tonight he will stay with me. He can sleep in Patrick's room."

Daisy's relief was profound and she spouted just a few more tears while expressing her gratitude. Before this moment he had been Dr. Denman or Patrick's father, but now she stood to cut through the Potter grounds to the Southern Pacific train station with her friend, Nicholas.

CHAPTER 16
Monday, August 23, 1909

When James Patillo arrived at the trackless trolley project site on Monday morning it was to find Sheriff Stewart leaning against the job shack awaiting his arrival. His gait faltered a moment and then he quickly adopted an air of hurried distraction, hoping the sheriff would understand he had little time for conversation at the start of a work day.

"Sheriff," he said, and shook Stewart's hand. "You're early at it."

"I guess you know why I'm here," the sheriff said.

Patillo tried to look innocent and answered, "Not really," then spat tobacco juice followed by the obligatory, "Sorry."

"I expect you heard about the fellow washed up on the beach at Castle Rock," Stewart said.

"Everyone has."

"Turns out he's a lawyer. He was working on something for this job you got going out here."

"If you say so." Patillo looked around, nervously twisting his moustache. The work crew was showing up now, and truth was, they pretty much knew what to do on their own, but he did his best to have the sheriff think he was needed. "You want to ask me something, Sheriff?"

"I met one of your workers on Saturday. He came to tell me he tripped over a dead man out here somewhere last Thursday night. You remember that at all?"

Patillo froze.

"He said you told him the guy was drunk, but he didn't believe it."

Patillo knew he was taking too long to respond, but was damned if he could think of anything to say. It seemed too late to feign total ignorance, but also unwise to admit anything.

"Let's go have a look at where the boy found the body," the sheriff continued, "and you can tell me what happened."

There was nothing for it but to go along. Patillo muttered something under his breath about needing to get to work, then took off walking in the direction of the laguna, the sheriff close behind him.

As they trudged across the mud bog, John Tade turned his Model T off Hubbard Avenue and pulled up to the job shack. When he brought the car to a stop, both Patillo and the sheriff turned to look at him. As soon as Tade spotted the badge on Stewart's chest his eyes went wide. He made a great pantomime of looking at his pocket watch and pretending to suddenly realize he was late for something. He tried to re-start his car in a hurry, but it was not so easily done. He was forced to run back and forth from the cab to the front of the car several times, first to retrieve the hand crank, then to turn the key back to its 'on' position, and once more to adjust the choke button. It took half-a-dozen cranks before the motor engaged, and by then the portly Tade was winded and sweating. He jumped into the driver's seat at last, executed a hasty three-point turn, then drove up the hill toward the country club.

"You know him?" the sheriff asked.

"He's my boss."

Stewart raised an eyebrow at the information, then the two turned back around and continued their trek. About ten yards from the lake in a particularly chaotic section of the track Patillo stopped, put his hands on his hips and turned in a circle to scan the surroundings. He said, "It was maybe around here someplace."

"Okay. You want to tell me what happened?"

"It's like the kid said, I guess. He was squawking and running around like he needed some help."

"Uh huh."

"There was a few of us saw him. Everyone came running."

"Who else?"

"I don't know. A carriage driver. Some other guy."

"Was anyone going to tell me about it?"

Patillo cleared his throat a couple of times, thinking. "Well, it was kind of a strange thing. I did tell Pimi the guy was drunk. I mean, he's just a kid. Then that carriage driver offered to take him and his mom on home."

Stewart nodded and Patillo relaxed just a bit. The sheriff must have heard the same from Pimi so maybe the little sliver of truth would give his whole story a leg up.

"The other fellow had a car so I asked if he could drive into town and notify the law. He said he would so I closed up the jobsite and when I came back, the body was gone. I guess I figured he took it with him."

Sheriff Stewart stared sightlessly over Patillo's head for a few moments. "I have to tell you," he finally said, "I'm having a hard time picturing it. A man you don't know loaded up a dead body that appeared out of nowhere and drove off with it, and you were good with that?"

"I know him," Patillo said, then couldn't stop his eyes from flicking in the direction of the club house.

"So, the other guy was your boss."

Patillo spat and looked at the ground.

"Any idea why he gave a dead man a trip to Castle Rock?"

"No."

"Well, I best have a word with him. What's his name?"

"John Tade, but I sure hope he won't think it's me causing him trouble."

"I can understand that."

"I better get to work," Patillo said, then he stepped around the sheriff and practically sprinted in the direction of a group of workers over by the incline.

The sheriff watched him go and allowed himself a smirk. That went well. Looked like James Patillo was in up to his tobacco-stained moustache. He shifted his gaze up to the Country Club and squinted at Tade's car. *No time like the present,* he thought to himself. He glanced around looking for Lois. The wily creature had stumbled upon a haystack near the job shack. He pulled her gently from the treasure trove, swung into the saddle, then coaxed her up the hill to the Country Club.

John Tade was watching through the window of the dining area as the sheriff dismounted and walked around the Model T a couple of times before heading up the stairs to come inside. Heart racing, he bolted down a hallway, through the kitchen and out the back door as fast as he could go. He left the door open a bit so he could listen inside, but all he could hear was the clanking of dishes and the clanging of pots and pans.

He waited for what seemed an eternity, then tiptoed out to the porch to see if he could catch site of the sheriff or his horse. When he poked his head around the corner, he immediately found himself face-to-face with Stewart who had been directed by the club staff to have a look out back.

"Morning," the sheriff said. "Is that your car out there?"

"Yes, yes it is," Tade answered energetically and plastered a smile on his face. "It's something, isn't it?"

"Yes, it is. By any chance, were you out here last Thursday?"

Tade had no way of knowing what Patillo had said to the sheriff. If it was already established he had been there and he said he wasn't, it would look bad.

"Let's see," he said, eyes tracking back and forth as he pretended to cogitate. "Was that the day of the tournament? Sure it was. Yes, I was here. Why do you ask?"

"Do you remember when you left?"

"Not exactly."

Both men fell silent, each determined that the other would speak next. After a full minute the sheriff extended his hand in introduction.

"Sorry, name's Nat Stewart."

"John Tade," came the reply, and the men shook hands. Then silence as Tade's mind spun frantically and the sheriff waited patiently.

Tade finally spoke, saying, "Now that you mention Thursday, I remember something a little strange as I was leaving."

"Oh?"

"Well, I was just giving the site a last look to make sure it was secure for the night before I went back to my hotel."

"You're part of this operation then?"

"Well, yeah - the whole thing was my idea."

"You don't say." The sheriff's expression made him seem more impressed than he actually was.

"Anyways, there was a commotion, and the foreman said some kid was scared to death of something he saw out there. I went to have a look, but I didn't see anything. Then I drove back to the hotel."

"That's it?"

"That's it."

"Did you go back and tell the foreman you didn't see anything?"

"Sure. Of course." Tade tried to squelch the panic rising in his throat.

The sheriff gazed out over the jobsite while Tade tried to relax his face, certain that he looked guilty as hell. Stewart started down the steps, then turned to ask, "Where you staying, Mr. Tade?"

"The Neal Hotel."

"All right then," Stewart said, and headed for his horse.

CHAPTER 17
Tuesday, August 24, 1909

Tuesday, the twenty-fourth of August, was Leontine's official birthday, but that was not her first thought upon waking. Her sleep had been fitful and filled with troubling dreams of murderous thieves.

Typically, she would rise immediately upon awakening and get busy with whatever tasks she had lined out for herself the night before as she fell into sleep. But today, she rolled onto her back, buried her eyes in the crook of her arm and allowed unsettling thoughts to surface.

Sunday night Innocencia had been made comfortable in the eldest daughter Aracadia's bed. She had fallen asleep almost immediately and slept heavily through the entire night. Though silent and withdrawn the following day, now that others were around, she at least seemed less agitated and fearful for Juan Carlos. Hermogenes' wife, Juana, had coaxed her into eating some beef broth and a few bites of applesauce which had provided a hint of color to her ashen face.

At the breakfast table Monday morning, the kids gushed excitedly about a plan to take Patrick along the creek bed that led to the beach a quarter-mile away where they could spend hours swimming and fishing and digging in the sand. Patrick kept his eyes on his ham and eggs. He glanced up at Leontine for just an instant, and in that brief moment she saw that he was afraid. She told them that she was sorry, but she was going to need Patrick's help with some things at Innocencia's, and promised that they would come back soon for a day dedicated to frolicking.

In the end, she was even more glad of the face-saving gesture than Patrick. They returned to the Barón rancho, along with Juan Carlos, and the three set about tasks of cleaning and airing that took most of the day. Leontine could not stop herself from comparing the desolation and emptiness of the adobe and outbuildings with the liveliness of her cousin's home – a liveliness she had experienced in the Barón home not so long ago.

By the time they returned, Juana had supper on the table. She surprised Leontine with a birthday cake after the meal, then they all gathered in the living room to commune in an atmosphere that felt almost like a holiday. Patrick enjoyed himself tremendously. The boys taught him to play checkers with a beautiful store-bought game board and checkers they carved themselves from small disks of wood. He loved the game and was eager to make a set of his own as soon as they got home.

Leontine, however, was haunted by Innocencia's forsaken home. As pleasant as the gathering was, she felt that she floated somewhere just outside it, worrying about Vincent's mother and the rest of his family. She revisited the horrific tale of the Mission San Miguél murders repeatedly in her mind and contemplated what, if anything, it had to do with Vincent's disappearance. She would tug her attention back to the world around her only to realize a short time later that she was again absorbed in events from the past. What was this obsession? What was to be gained from following endless threads of imaginings to their various invented outcomes? The world is as it is, however much we might wish it were not. She had proven to herself once, the way out of this trap was to embrace that she would never know what became of Vincent, but she was realizing now that, in truth, she had remained caught in the trap all along – and feared now that she might always be.

Leontine removed her arm from her eyes and let in the world around her. With a sigh, she at last remembered that today was her birthday. As a child her birthdays had been rather staid occasions. Her mother suffered terribly with depression and her anxious father always did his best to keep the immediate surroundings calm and subdued. Though Leontine's family and friends probably made as big a fuss for her as for anyone else through the years, the duty she felt as a child to ask for nothing and keep excitement at bay had apparently become cast in stone.

Weary of rumination, she finally rolled out of bed to prepare for the journey home. She shook the road dust out of her traveling suit as best she could. Innocencia's bath on Sunday had turned road grit to mud, now caked and embedded in the fabric. When she emerged from the bedroom at last, it was to find Patrick already dressed and fed. The boys had readied Lindy Sue and the carriage without having to be asked. After hugs and good-byes and promises of a quick return, Leontine and Patrick were on the road home by nine o'clock.

Patrick waited until they were alone to give Leontine her birthday present. He reached into his pocket and produced a nearly white stone, roughly the size of a lemon, that conformed perfectly with the palm of her hand. He had smoothed and polished the jagged rock with considerable effort and coaxed the natural curve of the stone into the sleek likeness of a resting dove. It was enchanting, and the shape and weight of it felt delicious in her hand. She loved it completely, and hoped she was able to communicate how moved and grateful she felt for the gift.

They made good time, with less sight-seeing and dallying, and it was just after three o'clock when Leontine returned the carriage to the Talley Ho, bade a fond farewell to Lindy Sue, then gratefully allowed Diego to carry her satchel across the street to her apartment while she walked Patrick home.

Dr. Denman was not yet home from work, but would no doubt show up soon. She went into the house with Patrick to say good-bye and make sure he felt safe, and they were both curious about a canvas duffel bag stashed inside the door, but there was no knowing about it at the moment.

When Leontine got back home, she ducked quickly into the store to let Uncle Remy know she had returned. He was engaged with a customer, so Leontine said briefly that she was tired and hungry and going upstairs to eat and freshen up, and that they would chat later. Remy started to reply, but was interrupted by his impatient customer. Too tired to wait, Leontine retreated and headed upstairs.

Remy had actually been about to tell her that someone was in her apartment waiting for her, but Leontine knew it anyway before she reached the top of the stairs. Victoria was up there and had busied herself in the kitchen. Oh, heavenly day. Leontine could smell colorado sauce simmering on the stove. There was shredded pork keeping warm in one of the ovens until it would be mixed with the Guajillo chili and tomato puree, minced garlic, salt and lard, rolled into one of the fresh tortillas piled and warming on the center griddle tray, then sprinkled with diced onions and cilantro. Leontine's mouth watered in anticipation. The women greeted with a warm embrace, and Victoria bestowed heartfelt wishes for health and happiness in honor of Leontine's birthday.

Leontine went to her room to remove her hat and change out of her grimy traveling suit, splash her face, and freshen her upswept hair before returning to the kitchen to dive into the feast. As she ate, closing her eyes to experience the deliciousness of nearly every bite, Leontine recounted the enjoyable evening spent with her extended family. She also shared her deep concern for Innocencia and her frail condition, skipping over the tale of the Mission San Miguél murders and Vincent's frightening half-brother. That was for another time. Then, having finished the eating and the telling, Leontine watched the back of Victoria as she cleaned the dishes and put them away. Even from behind, Leontine could see and feel tension in the woman's movement.

Leontine said, "Here I am chatting along and have not even asked about you."

"Estoy bien, mija," Victoria answered without turning around, and she shrugged her shoulders.

"Victoria, please tell me. What's wrong?"

With a sigh Victoria dried her hands on a kitchen towel, then took a seat across the table from Leontine. She folded her hands in front of her and studied them closely for several moments. Finally, meeting Leontine's eyes, she said, "I promised to be silent, but have talked it over with Jesus. He thinks I'm over my own head."

Leontine smiled inwardly at the attempted use of the idiom. "We'll keep the secret together," she said.

"The little baby. He is Margarita's son," Victoria said as a tear escaped and trailed down her cheek.

"Is Francis Fordyce the father?"

"No. Not yet. He was going to adopt him."

"I see."

"But then he died."

"Yes."

"And the lady still wants the baby because then she will have money. But Margarita knows the lady is cold. She does not want her for Frankie."

"Understandably."

"But now the lady says she will tell the law that Justito had something to do with the death of the man unless Margarita will release her baby."

"Oh dear."

"Justito was there when they say the man died. I fear someone will believe it because he is so often angry – but they don't know him."

"So, he did die in Hope Ranch." Leontine said, remembering that Sheriff Stewart had suspected as much before she left for Gaviota.

"He had electrocution," Victoria said, which caused Leontine to wince as she thought of Patrick's reaction to the sight of the dead man's hands. It must have been horrible.

"Your children are good and strong, Victoria – as you have raised them. I know you will worry whatever I say, but we can believe they will proceed in whatever manner is best."

"You can believe. I will pray," her friend responded.

Several moments passed, then Victoria rose from the table saying she would go across the street to ask her nephew Diego to take her home. Leontine walked with her down the stairs and watched from the doorway as she crossed the street to the Tally Ho. It was not until she returned to the apartment that she realized her thoughts were directing themselves toward the unfortunate incident, freed for the moment from the pull of the past. It was a relief and she vowed she would continue to hold her thoughts in the present, where they might actually do some good, even if only as witness to the concerns of a friend.

CHAPTER 18

Nicholas closed the door behind his last patient of the day, walked to his desk, and sank into his chair with a sigh. He was eager to get home to see his son and hear about the visit with Leontine's cousins, but first he just needed a minute. His eyes drifted to the window, though he did not focus on anything outside it. He replayed his parting with Pearl earlier in the day in his mind, combing through the exchange to be certain he had said all that was necessary. It was cumbersome to address a circumstance never acknowledged aloud. All he could think to do was make encouraging comments about the position at the Bancroft and hope the larger context was understood. Though her smile remained bright and their farewell embrace was warm, the tilt of her head and stiffness in her posture as she boarded the train left an impression of someone determined to appear unshaken. He could feel the same stance in himself. Time would tell. He heaved another great sigh.

It was then that he heard a light tap on the office door, and he felt a flash of annoyance. He needed to get home. He had instructed Daisy's brother to be away from the house until dinnertime so that Patrick would not come home to a stranger, and so he would have a chance to explain a little something about their guest before introducing him to his son. But on the other side of the door someone was sick or in pain or frightened for someone else who was, so he forced himself out of his chair and opened his office door.

To his surprise he found the young Widow Fordyce dressed in her mourning frock and looking tearful, embarrassed and scared. He felt immediately chagrined about his thought from the day before that she might be an uncaring mother or anything other than a lost soul cast suddenly adrift. He invited her in, waving her protests of intrusion aside, and directed her to the chair facing his across the desk. Before she began speaking, Mrs. Fordyce took a handkerchief from its hiding place in her sleeve, then clasped her hands on top of his desk and took a breath to collect herself before she began to speak.

"Thank you for seeing me Dr. Denman," she said. "I don't know where else to turn. Francis was always the one to advise me, and now I don't…" Her eyes filled with tears and she raised the handkerchief to capture them.

Nicholas leaned forward in his chair, keeping his eyes on her face and suppressing an urge to reach across the desk to comfort her.

"I received a telegram this afternoon," Caroline continued. "It was from my husband's business partner. Among other things, he asks when I will return to Los Angeles, and when Francis can be taken…sent…as well. I can't even think who to ask," she said, and dabbed at her tears some more.

"It will all sort itself out in time, Mrs. Fordyce. Please try to focus on yourself and your son for now."

"I know you're right, Doctor, but Francis and I have not been married long. I don't know what is expected of me, or whom to trust."

"No one can force you to do anything. Send them away and say you are under a doctor's care for now. It's true. You need to spend time with your baby, Mrs. Fordyce. I'm sure he can sense that something is terribly wrong."

Caroline did not respond right away and looked into her lap for several moments. Nicholas waited, certain there was something more that was troubling her. Finally, she asked, "May I confide in you, Doctor? It's a bit of a delicate matter."

"Of course."

She seemed reluctant to continue, then finally admitted, "Frankie is actually Margaret's baby. We were in the process of adopting him."

"I see," Nicholas said. That explained plenty.

"We thought that coming to Santa Barbara would be good for Margaret, so she could draw support and comfort from her family. I never expected them to try to convince her to keep Frankie. Her brother quarreled with Francis. Are you familiar with Margaret's brother?"

"I can't say I am."

"I hate to admit it, but I find him quite intimidating. Without Francis to stand up to him I'm frightened I'll lose Frankie, too."

"Where is Frankie now?"

"With Margaret. I don't know what to do," Caroline said, blinking back more tears.

"I wish I had an answer for you, Mrs. Fordyce, but I'm far from an expert in legal matters. Please know I will help you any way I can.".

"It helps just to say these things out loud." Caroline rose from her chair and continued, "I've taken enough of your time. Thank you for helping me to feel less alone."

"You are not alone," Nicholas replied, and he rose as well. He walked her to the door with assurances that he would look in on her the following morning. Once she was gone, a quick glance at the clock showed ten minutes after five, and Nicholas grabbed his hat and left his office for home.

Caroline emerged from the Eddy Building onto State Street marveling, not for the first time, at the ease with which men could be manipulated. She had planted the seed of doubt against Margaret's brother, and felt certain she had gained an ally in her quest for possession of Francis Fordyce, III. She stepped into her hired carriage, then directed the driver to Rancheria Street. She wanted a look at the living arrangements of the Ramirez household so she could arrive at a reasonably enticing dollar amount to offer the family in order to help convince Margaret that the adoption was her best choice. Caroline was fairly certain no amount would sway Margaret herself, but the right number could well turn her family against her. She had a feeling it wouldn't take much at all.

It was a quarter past five when Daisy arrived home, delighted to find Leontine in the living room with the latest edition of Harper's Bazar magazine and a much-needed cup of tea. Each woman was so full of news it was difficult to know who should go first or where to begin. In the end, Leontine made a cup of tea for Daisy and another for herself, then recounted the visit with Patrick much as she had just done for Victoria - leaving out any reference to Vincent or the stories told by Innocencia. She did say to Daisy that there was more to tell, but that she was eager to be brought up to date on events in Santa Barbara and would fill her in later.

"Victoria mentioned the victim was electrocuted in Hope Ranch."

"How did she know about that?"

"She didn't say."

"Nicholas assisted in the autopsy just yesterday. The sheriff was going out to Hope Ranch today to have a look around. I found information about the foreman in an old newspaper, and haven't even had a chance to tell him about it yet. We need to all get together again so we can catch each other up."

"I agree."

After several moments, Daisy surprised her friend by saying, "That's not all. My brother has come to town with plans to take me back to San Francisco."

Leontine blinked and set down her tea. "My goodness," she said.

"He stayed with Nicholas last night."

"Really. How long will he be in town?"

"I suppose as long as it takes to convince me."

The women's eyes met, then Leontine said, "Quite some time I should think." They fell silent, staring into their individual teacups until Leontine continued, "He can stay in the other room here if you like. There's nothing in there but clothing."

"I don't know," Daisy said. But it was obvious to both of them that imposing on Nicholas was not the answer. They quickly readied the room, and then themselves, for a walk to the Denman home.

When they arrived there just after six-thirty, Nicholas and Patrick were finishing up a light dinner of creamed chicken on toast. Leontine showed off the birthday gift from Patrick that she had thought to tuck into her clasped needlepoint handbag. Nicholas and Daisy marveled at the curved and polished stone, lavishing Patrick with praise for his effort. Not long after, there came another knock at the door, and Patrick ran to meet Will and let him inside. Will was fond of children and listened intently as Patrick described his trip up the coastline and the playing of checkers, and Will offered his opinion about the best materials from which to fashion a game board and playing pieces.

Leontine extended the offer of her third bedroom - she and Daisy both expressing their gratitude to Nicholas for putting Will up the night before. The offer was readily accepted, Will no doubt hopeful that the longer he had his sister's attention, the better his chances of bringing her around to his way of thinking.

Nicholas then turned their attention to the project Patrick would share at the exhibition table at the End-of-Summer Carnival the following day. With Patrick, the challenge had not been to complete a project in time, but to decide which one of his projects would be best to display. Nicholas had nominated his repair and refinishing of a cast-iron mechanical bank.

The toy was in the form of a magician standing on a small stage behind a table, and holding a top hat out in front of him. When one placed a coin in the center of the table and pressed a lever, the hat lowered to cover the coin. It would then "disappear", sliding down a difficult-to-detect chute, and into a holding chamber. When the lever was released the magician raised the hat again to reveal an empty table. Patrick found the toy underneath the wooden bleachers at the athletic field one day, no doubt discarded by its former owner as the mechanics were no longer working.

Patrick felt a little bit like a cheater because it had been so easy to free a coin trapped in the chute, then freshen up the painted surfaces. It had taken him no more than an hour to complete the whole project. Leontine suggested that he bring along a small bag of pennies so other children could give it a go. All agreed it was a splendid idea, and it was arranged that he would come by the market in the morning for a supply of them.

Though the desire to discuss advancements in the solving of the mystery surrounding Francis Fordyce was present, if unspoken, the women wanted to get Will settled in the spare bedroom for the night. As they parted, all agreed that an early dinner at the Potter the following day was in order, and Daisy volunteered to contact Sheriff Stewart to make sure he was included. It had been a long day for everyone, and all would be early to bed.

CHAPTER 19
Wednesday, August 25, 1909

֍

The End-of-Summer Carnival saw all of Alameda Park set up for
games, competitions, exhibitions and presentations. There were now six
elementary schools in Santa Barbara and, as a result, this year the carnival
had been expanded to a two-day celebration. The first day centered
mainly around the younger kids and focused on group activities like
sing-alongs, and simpler games such as tag, leap frog and hide-and-seek.
On the second day, older children engaged in more competitive games
including tug-of-war, sack racing and ring tossing, and their exhibitions
were not just displayed, but judged and awarded ribbons.

The Sola Street side of the park contained makeshift booths erected
for more elaborate games. One could "rent" a fishing pole for a penny,
which was actually nothing more than a stick with some string wound
around the end of it. The string was lowered into the booth where another
child, crouching inside, would attach a small toy or penny candy with a
clothes pin, then give it a tug indicating the prize was "caught". In another
booth, one could toss a small canvas bag filled with rice onto a flat table
top with a target painted on its top. The owner of the bag that landed
closest to the bullseye would win a prize.

Plank tables lining the Micheltorena Street side of the park defined
the exhibition area and displayed projects children had pursued over the
course of the summer. Those awarded blue ribbons were placed on the
"Winner's Table" inside the gazebo. Several wooden benches were situated
in rows in front of the gazebo for viewing presentations by musical or
singing groups that gathered on the stairs to perform throughout the day.

Tables along the Anacapa Street side of the park were stocked with
large quantities of paper, pencils and Crayola crayons. Finished pictures
were pinned to a board for judging and the awarding of ribbons. Food

tables lined the Santa Barbara Street side, loaded primarily with cookies, cakes and pies. Kids ran around in packs while any parents in attendance gathered in the center of the park to visit, meet teachers, or simply watch and enjoy.

When Patrick arrived with his magician bank and bag of pennies, he was perplexed to immediately find himself the center of attention. He had planned to make a brief appearance and watch from the sidelines for a short while in a technical adherence to his father's wishes. Because of the report in Monday's *Daily Independent*, however, classmates and teachers alike were eager to hear details about his discovery of the dead man on the beach at Castle Rock.

Attention was not something young Patrick was prepared to deal with, most especially about an event that had left him feeling so weak, and in very short order he'd had enough of it. Groups of children that normally had nothing to do with him called to him to include him in their little circles of exclusivity. For some reason it made him mad. He avoided them all as best he could, and before the women of the Civic League had even laid out the lunch feast, he sneaked off and headed for the safety of the adobe. Once arrived, he put the mechanical bank and pennies aside and set about the business of rounding up materials for his checkerboard.

Patrick's behavior did not go unnoticed, and one of his former teachers sent an older student to Dr. Denman's office with a note expressing her concern. Nicholas immediately contacted a local nurse, Mrs. Annie Daggett, to come to his office to see his afternoon patients, help those she could, and reschedule or refer out any that needed more assistance than she could provide. Then he made his way to the old adobe.

Patrick was no more surprised to see his dad walk in the door at one o'clock in the afternoon than Nicholas was to find him there. They spent a couple of hours fashioning wooden squares, some from exceedingly hard and reddish-colored manzanita wood, and some from softer pine wood that Patrick planned to paint black. He would glue them all together on a wooden tray fashioned to hold the checkerboard squares in the center, with a section for holding the checkers built into each end. It would take quite some time to complete, but they made a good start.

As was so often the case, Patrick and his father did not speak directly about any of the upsetting issues at hand, but the calm and connection of working together on the project left the boy feeling much more himself. When Nicholas reminded him that they were meeting Leontine, Daisy and the sheriff at the Potter for an early dinner, Patrick was delighted, feeling more than ready to venture out into the world again.

Leontine spent the day at the market. She told Uncle Remy about the trip to Uncle Hermogenes', and showed him the dove Patrick had made for her birthday. Remy gave her his present then – a spanking new copy of one of his favorite dime novels: *The Virginian* by Owen Wister. The rhythm and flow of the market was a familiar comfort, and Leontine felt a contentment that had eluded her for several days as she tended to the accounts and spruced up the window display. She wondered several times how Daisy was faring with her brother. It was difficult to imagine that her friend and tenant could possibly leave, but family is family and for some it is a duty impossible to reject.

In fact, waking up under the same roof had put the siblings immediately at odds. They had barely finished breakfast before the hollering started. There was only Daisy staying put or going back with no avenue for compromise. Will swore he was not leaving without her. Daisy noted the little ones were only in a worse boat without him. She said his point was made and there was no reason for him to stare at her while she tried to make up her mind. Will reasoned that he could perhaps hurry things along by reminding her hourly what a spoiled, selfish brat she was being, and she reminded him that he was not now, and had never been, in a position to tell her what to do. These points were made at top volume and included some wall punching and a few tears.

Finally, Daisy said she needed to get to work and suggested that her brother sit in the apartment and rot for all she cared. She walked the three blocks to the paper at top speed in an effort to burn off her frustration.

O'Brien saw her enter the office, flop into her desk chair, then proceed to scowl into the space in front of her. He waited a good long while before calling her into his office. He didn't know exactly what to say, but figured if it seemed best, he could encourage her to talk to him about what was troubling her and maybe feel a little better, or at the very least, prevail on her to stop moping and get some work done.

When he finally did summon her, she stomped into his office and flopped into the chair facing him, arms crossed and expression challenging, as if he were the adversary in the whole situation.

"Owen sent a note that he wants to see you," O'Brien said.

"Why?"

"He didn't say."

"His two legs are broken, I guess. Why can't he come over here?"

O'Brien nodded. She was just a little bit scary.

"I don't see why I have to always be the one kowtowing to everybody else," she continued at increased volume. "I don't see why other people can't just – just – " then she burst into tears.

O'Brien checked his pocket for a handkerchief, but since there was never one there, it would be surprising to find one now. Without any awareness of what she was doing, Daisy took care of the situation herself, wiping her cheeks with the hem of her skirt. O'Brien tried not to smile, finding the act kind of adorable for some reason. He said, "Until you get things settled in your mind, I don't think you're going to be much use for anything else."

"Thank you very much, but I already have enough people telling me what I should do."

"I'm not telling you what to do."

Silent glare.

"If you want to spit and spin and mope and wail, go right ahead." Daisy's eyes narrowed, but at least she wasn't crying anymore.

"Tell me something," O'Brien continued. "Do you like working here?"

"You know I do."

"Better than what you had going on up north?"

"Of course, but so what? What kind of mother leaves her children on their own because she finds something she likes better?"

"Are they your children?"

"No, but…" Agitated, Daisy rose from the chair and moved behind her boss to stare out the window. "They're not mine, and they are. I don't know if you can understand," she said. "I can save them."

O'Brien stood also, and went to face Daisy as he spoke to her gently. "You don't know what life has lined up for someone else, Daisy. People find their way. It's not your job to save them."

"Are you sure?" she asked.

"Of course not."

That made her smile, and she lightly smacked him on the arm.

"Now, go see what Owen wants. He made it sound like you'd be excited about whatever he's got."

Daisy lowered her eyes, feeling a little sheepish. "Okay," she said, but didn't move.

"Go on," O'Brien said, and when she looked up they stood in front of the window looking into each other's eyes for nearly a full minute. When she left the room, it seemed somehow deflated, and Tom O'Brien finally admitted to himself just how much more he liked it when Daisy Merrie was nearby.

When Daisy swung into the Stafford Saloon, it took her eyes a few moments to adjust to the dim light. Not that she needed light to know where Reed was sitting. She walked over to the short end of the bar and slid onto the stool next to him. All things considered, it seemed like a good time for a beer, and she ordered one from the bartender.

Resting on the bar in front of Reed was a Derby hat caked with dirt and dried mud. Reed scooted it in her direction using his whiskey glass.

"What's this?"

"A little something I found on my stool this morning."

"Do tell." Daisy picked up the hat for closer inspection and saw that, besides looking as if it had been rolled in the dirt, it seemed also to have been torched around the inside rim.

"Someone wants to be sure we know how the lawyer died," Reed said.

"Agreed. Should I take it to the sheriff?"

"May as well."

"Any guess who left it?"

"Nope."

Daisy slid off the stool just as the bartender delivered her beer. She locked eyes with Reed and kept them there while she downed nearly the entire glass, set what little was left on the bar, then wiped her mouth with her sleeve. Reed smirked and lifted his glass to her as she spun out of the place to seek out the sheriff with her prize.

She found him in his office working on a cup of coffee and ruminating about the very subject of her call. This was her first opportunity to report her discovery of the connection between Patillo and Fordyce from the lawsuit in Glendale. She also told him about Patillo's visit to Owen Reed at the Stafford to proclaim innocence in advance about anything bad that might occur in the future. Then she set the hat on the desk and Stewart picked it up to examine.

"What's this?"

"Someone left it on Owen's stool. I think it belonged to Fordyce."

"I expect you're right."

"Whoever left it had to have been out at Hope Ranch."

"Yep," Stewart said, and then he stood up from his desk and got his own hat, a tan Stetson he'd worn for ten years at least, and prepared for yet another trip to Hope Ranch. "You coming?" he asked.

"I don't want to slow you down," Daisy admitted. Her horsemanship was decidedly lacking. She'd had no use for a horse getting around in San Francisco and, though she could ride around town if necessary, the trek to Hope Ranch seemed daunting. "I'll find you out there," she said.

Within the hour Daisy was queued up with four guests of the Potter who were heading out to the country club in the hotel motorbus. Two were businessmen visiting from the mid-west and the others a wealthy older couple from Sacramento, in Santa Barbara for a holiday. Technically, the motorbus was intended only for hotel guests, something Daisy, dressed in her typical white linen shirt and cotton skirt, could hardly be mistaken for. But when she approached the visitors with her notebook and a winning smile, and introduced herself as a reporter for the local newspaper who was wondering if they had anything to say about their stay in Santa Barbara, the group was only too happy to include her in their excursion. The bus driver let her sit beside him in the front seat and she spent the entire journey facing backwards so she could chat with the sightseers.

By the time the group arrived at the country club, Sheriff Stewart was already down near the laguna with Patillo and John Tade, too. She parted company with her traveling companions and walked down the slope toward the men. When she got to them, the sheriff introduced her as the one who had brought him Fordyce's hat.

"So, this is where they found the body," the sheriff said, indicating an area a few feet from the mud bog. "And over there," he continued, pointing to a spot between where they were standing and the job shack, "is where Mr. Patillo here says a piece of equipment has gone missing."

"This is the first I've heard about it," Tade interjected.

"What was it?" Daisy asked.

"An electrical transformer," Patillo said, then spit tobacco juice, and muttered "sorry" under his breath.

"What was it supposed to do?" the sheriff asked.

"Fluctuate the current to make it harder for the trolley to get through the bog and up the incline," Patillo explained. "We have to stress the system to test it."

Daisy and the sheriff looked around the project with new understanding. The work in process actually made at least a little bit of sense now.

"Was something wrong with it?" the sheriff asked.

"Not that I know of," Patillo said, "He had it wired and we were going to hoist it onto the support beam between the poles today."

"Who's 'he'?"

"The Edison fellow. He should have been here hours ago."

"You know his name?"

"No, but he's the one that runs the company."

The sheriff turned to Daisy. "That's right next door to your paper," he said. "You ever meet him?"

"I've seen him. I think it's T. J. - or something J."

"Guess I'll find out." Then the sheriff turned to Patillo and Tade and said, "Let's talk about Thursday night."

Tade and Patillo's eyes met for a split second. Neither knew exactly what the other had already said.

"Mr. Tade, I remember Mr. Patillo here saying he told you to drive into town to let me know about the body, but I can't remember exactly – is that what you said you did?" Stewart continued.

"Well, no. I was – uh…It was so late."

The sheriff nodded, eyes focused on the horizon and looking as though he was thinking it over. Finally, he said, "Oh, now I remember. You said you didn't see anything and went on back to your hotel."

Patillo whirled on Tade. "That ain't the truth and you know it!" he said. "He saw it same as me!"

Daisy smiled inwardly. She had never actually witnessed the sheriff in action like this.

"Well, now that we're all here together, why don't we see if we can piece it together?" Stewart suggested.

With much hemming and hawing, the two explained how important it was to finish installing the prototype before the arrival of Ned Harriman the following week. They were worried he might pull the plug on the whole project if it was not fully operational when he got there. They admitted to throwing the body from the cliff so it would turn up someplace else and give them time to finish, stressing the point once again that the man was already dead when they found him.

"You're not taking us to jail, are you?" Patillo asked.

"Let's just say you're a long way from out of the woods."

"Sheriff, Fordyce and us were on the same side. He was trying real hard to keep things going," Tade said.

"There's another side?" Daisy asked.

"I know someone that would be happy if it failed," Tade answered.

"Who would that be?" the sheriff asked.

"Another one of the lawyers, name of Lovell. He hates this project. Always has. And he wasn't too fond of Mr. Fordyce either."

"Would he take that piece of equipment?"

"I doubt he'd know even one thing about it," Patillo said.

"I'm just saying, if you're looking for someone who would be happy about the way things are coming around, the only one I can think of is him," Tade said.

"Okay, I take your point," the sheriff said. "You know where he's staying?"

"The Potter," Tade said. "He's there most of the time – even if we need him here."

With that, Sheriff Stewart told both men to let him know if anything else came to mind, and not to go anywhere because he'd be wanting another chat with them about the whole tossing the body into the ocean business. Then he walked off to separate Lois from the haystack, ride back into town, and see if he could find the fellow at the Edison Company.

Daisy told John Tade she'd like to hear more about the trolley project, and asked if he might give her a ride back to town in his car. Tade wasn't about to say 'no' to anything she asked. His car was parked up by the country club and he offered to fetch it and come back to get her. It created the perfect opportunity for a minute alone with James Patillo.

"You said you didn't know Fordyce," Daisy said to Patillo, once Tade was out of earshot.

"Not really. I'd see him out here sometimes, but he's not really part of the construction." Patillo spat, forgetting that he was now only in the company of a woman. "Sorry," he said, meaning it this time.

"I should tell you before you say anything more that I know it was his law firm that beat you in the lawsuit with the city of Glendale."

Patillo looked stunned. "I don't know what you're talking about," he protested. "I mean, I know what you're talking about, but I never met him."

"I know. I'm saying it was his law firm that represented the city."

"I never saw him or anything. I swear it. I didn't even know."

"You understand why I mention it."

"I guess it could look bad, but you have to believe me."

"What about Mr. Tade?"

"What about him? I don't really know the man, but I don't know why he'd hurt the guy that was doing him the most good."

On the drive back to Santa Barbara, Daisy heard from John Tade about the ins and outs and ups and downs of the trackless trolley. She asked him to say more about what Lovell might have to gain from the death of Fordyce.

"He was Harriman's favorite until this project came along," Tade said. "If you ask me, he thought Fordyce was after his job."

"What about Mr. Patillo?" Daisy asked.

"What about him? I don't even know the man. But I do know the last thing he wants is for the project to stop."

Interesting, Daisy thought. The responses were so similar it made them seem rehearsed.

The two fell silent after that and in ten minutes more Tade dropped Daisy off in front of the Birabent Market. She would change into her green silk skirt and best linen shirt, then head to the Potter ahead of the others. She planned to secure their table and use the extra time to make some notes. She always thought more clearly once she put pen to paper.

CHAPTER 20

At a quarter past five Leontine removed her apron and closed up the register for the day, Uncle Remy having left earlier with a plan to stop at Faulding's Bookstore to check for any new or used novels that may have arrived. She would need to change into something nicer for dinner. She folded the apron and tucked it into the shelf under the counter, then looked up to see Hermogenes walk in the door. She rounded the counter to greet him, seeing by the look on his face he was carrying heavy news.

"I thought you would want to know," he said. "I think we've lost Innocencia. Whatever devil is in her head has taken over. She doesn't know what's going on around her anymore."

"I'm so sorry to hear it."

"She's already gone to Tina's. Gloria said she'll be fine with the baby and would rather her sister take care of their mom."

"What about the farm?"

"Her ranch hand Antonio can deal with the orchard, but the house – I don't know. Juan Carlos says he can take care of everything. He has been anyway. It'll probably be easier with his mother gone, but he'll be alone. Juana says we should bring him in with us, but then I worry about the place if no one is there."

The two tried to think of anyone who might be able to incorporate the maintenance of the farm north of Goleta into their lives, but the distance made things difficult. Ultimately it was a problem for the Barón family to resolve, but with the sisters both in Santa Maria, Juan Carlos so young and Vincent so long gone, the family might have no alternative but to sell the place.

"What of the half-brother?" Leontine asked.

"Whose half-brother?"

"Vincent's. I think there's an older brother."

"I've never heard of him."

Leontine wondered then if any of the story Innocencia had so urgently shared with her was true at all. The cousins parted with a promise to think about the situation, then she hurried upstairs to change.

Leontine felt too gloomy for her finer gowns and chose instead a more understated navy wrap dress with flared skirt, matching hat and a pink-pearl silk blouse.

She took the trolley to the Potter and entered the dining room shortly before six to find Daisy already at their table with her notebook. As they waited for Patrick, Nicholas and the sheriff to arrive, Daisy told her with some excitement of how the sheriff had allowed her to tag along when he went to question Patillo and Tade at the job site. There was more to tell, but she said she should wait for the others so the story would not be told twice. Leontine debated internally whether to divulge the information about young Frankie's heritage. Despite her promise to Victoria, she was beginning to think that sharing it might be the best course. "There is another angle I think we must consider," she said. "It may have nothing to do with the project in Hope Ranch at all."

"Do tell," Daisy said. But then their conversation was interrupted by the arrival of Patrick and Nicholas.

Though the temperature outside was still warm the four decided on soup and fresh bread more from convention than anything else, and all felt certain the sheriff would agree once he joined them. This evening's offering was a hearty pea soup with bits of carrot, turnip and generous chunks of salt pork. As they waited for their meal to be served they learned about the Denmans' progress with the checkerboard.

Nicholas asked about Will, and Daisy admitted she had successfully been avoiding him.

"Why? What's wrong with him?" Patrick asked.

"He wants me to move back to San Francisco and I don't want to go."

"I don't want you to go either," Patrick said. The table was silent for a moment as they all looked at Daisy. It was simply impossible to imagine her gone.

It was at that moment that Sheriff Stewart arrived. He removed his hat, slid into his chair and hung the Stetson from his right knee. He apologized for being late, explaining that he had stopped to tuck a note into the Edison Company door asking the manager to contact him as soon as possible. He and Daisy then shared the new revelations passed on by Patillo and Tade at the job site: the tossing of poor Mr. Fordyce into the waves, the missing piece of electrical equipment and their shared suspicion of a man named Lovell.

When the food arrived, conversation stopped immediately and they turned their collective attention to the meal. Because of the early hour the dining room was fairly empty, and in the relative quiet they easily overheard the maître d' address a dapper gentleman in tie and tails that he was seating two tables away. He asked, "Will someone be joining you, Mr. Lovell?" and the man replied that, yes, someone would be.

The five stopped chewing simultaneously. After several moments, Daisy turned to the sheriff and said, "One of us has to go over there."

"You go," Stewart said, tucking a napkin into his shirt collar to cover his badge. "I don't want him to think he's got trouble with the law just yet."

Daisy stood, smoothed her skirt, and headed for Lovell's table. She was nearly upon him before he looked up to see her. She smiled coyly and all but curtseyed in front of him.

"Excuse me, Mr. Lovell," she said, "but there's a newspaper reporter here who would love to have a word with you if you wouldn't mind." Then she watched as his eyes moved around her to look at her dining companions, attempting to assess which one of them might be the reporter.

"What on earth for?" Lovell asked, then added, "Tell him 'no.'"

"It's just that people know something is going on out in Hope Ranch. You know, since that's where that dead body came from and everything. They're curious."

Lovell was an attorney and former judge and recognized baiting when he heard it. This woman was fishing. He said, "I'm meeting someone. I'm afraid he'll have to find me another time." Then he dipped his head dismissively and turned his eyes to his menu.

"Maybe there's someone else to talk to."

"I don't know who that would be."

"Did you know the man? The one who died?"

Lovell lowered his menu and focused on the girl in front of him. Obviously, she herself was the reporter and thought she knew something, which was ever so slightly disquieting, but he would be damned if he'd let her engage him.

"Young lady," he said in his most condescending tone, "if you want an appointment with me, you will have to arrange it through my office. Now good day to you." With that he again looked at his menu.

"That's okay," Daisy chirped. "Between the foreman, Mr. Tade and the man from the Edison Company, we probably have all we need. Enjoy your dinner." Then she turned and went back to her friends. When she took her seat, she asked if he had watched her go.

"I'd say you got his attention," the sheriff said.

Nicholas was the one with the best view of the man and he was finding it difficult to stop himself from looking over at him. Each time he did he saw that Lovell was monitoring their table. Because they knew they could be overheard, Leontine asked Patrick to tell them about the carnival. Lovell soon lost interest in their conversation, but they still couldn't discuss the very matter that had brought them together without worrying he might hear. Once the soup was finished the sheriff excused himself, saying he should get home to his family and that they would no doubt all connect the following day.

Nicholas had just said 'yes' to Patrick's request for chocolate cake when Robert Lovell's dinner companion arrived. It was Caroline Fordyce, managing somehow to look quite alluring, despite her mourning dress. As she passed by their table she caught sight of Nicholas and smiled. He half-rose from his seat and dipped his head in greeting, then sat down to face inquisitive stares from both Leontine and Daisy.

Daisy said, "Well that's a pair to draw to," tilting her head in the direction of Caroline and Lovell.

"What do you mean by that?" Nicholas asked.

"I mean we've been lead to believe Mr. Lovell and Mr. Fordyce were not on good terms."

"No doubt she has legal issues to resolve. I'm sure he's a fine attorney if nothing else."

Daisy shot a sidelong look at Leontine. Was she hearing the testiness in Nicholas' voice?

"I'm sure you're right," Leontine said. "One can only hope those on the opposing side are as well advised."

"I'm not sure what you mean," Nicholas said, "but surely not that you would wish hardship for a young widow."

"One can be made a widow, Dr. Denman, and not made a saint."

"A harsh judgment, Miss Birabent. You surprise me," Nicholas replied with obvious irritation.

The tension at the table was impossible to mistake. Fortunately, the waiter appeared and made a great show of presenting Patrick with his chocolate cake. The few minutes were enough for Nicholas' defensive ire to diminish and for the flush of annoyance to leave Leontine's face. Both Daisy and Patrick were looking back and forth between the two. Leontine and Nicholas kept their eyes away from one another.

"What's going on?" Patrick asked, his voice coming out at a higher pitch than expected. He held a spoon in his hand, but had yet to take a bite of his cake.

"Nothing, Son," Nicholas said. "Sometimes people accidentally speak without knowing the circumstances."

"They do indeed," Leontine said, and she stood from her chair. "Please excuse me."

In her haste to leave the table, Leontine took her linen napkin with her, something she failed to notice until she was out on the front porch of the hotel. It became useful, however, with the appearance of indignant tears. It had been ages since she'd cried, and Leontine felt a panic in her throat that if she started now she might not be able to stop. She sat on one of the rocking chairs battling the urge with slow, deliberate breaths, and tried to focus on the ocean to calm herself.

Inside at the table, Patrick was having an equally hard time suppressing his tears. He didn't understand why Leontine was upset, but he knew his father was the cause. He turned angrily to his dad and shouted, "What did you say to her?" Without waiting for an answer, he jumped up from the table and hurried to find his friend.

Daisy sat back in her chair. She had no idea what just happened either. She silently kept her eyes on Nicholas and waited for him to look up from his lap. He wiped his mouth with his napkin, then laid it carefully on the table and finally met Daisy's look.

"That was interesting," Daisy said. "Are you all right?"

Nicholas felt chagrined, but his recent experience with the vulnerable young widow had stirred a protectiveness in him. He knew it was unlike

Leontine to snipe, but his reaction had been spontaneous. He shook his head, saying, "I should go find her."

"Give it a minute," Daisy suggested. "Maybe a short whiskey." Nicholas nodded his head wearily and signaled the waiter.

Patrick found Leontine on the porch in short order. He stood in front of her, his young face creased with concern. He wanted desperately to sit on her lap, but knew he was too old for that. He felt great relief when she scooted as far as she could to one side of her chair. He squeezed in next to her and pushed his glasses up on his nose.

"What's wrong?" he asked, sliding his hand into hers.

"Oh…a great many things, I'm afraid." More of the tears she was working so hard to suppress spilled from her eyes.

"Did my dad hurt your feelings?"

"A little bit," she confessed. The two sat in silence for a minute, then Leontine took another deep breath.

"You can tell me," Patrick said. "He makes me mad sometimes."

Leontine smiled then. "I'll tell you my troubles if you tell me yours," she proposed.

Patrick thought it over for a moment, then said, "Okay."

"Will you go first?"

Patrick heaved a great sigh. Somewhat to his own surprise, he admitted to Leontine that he was a big baby. He described for her in detail his discovery of the body and his shame over his reaction. He admitted that he felt afraid of the water now, and even that he had started to feel afraid of the dark. He didn't want to tell his dad because he was afraid he would be disappointed and he didn't want him to worry. He felt afraid almost all the time and didn't know what to do about it. "I just want to go back to normal," he said, and in that moment realized that, for the first time in nearly a week, he did feel normal.

Leontine removed her hand from Patrick's and wrapped her arm around his shoulder, drawing him close. They enjoyed the calm for a bit, then Patrick wiped his cheeks and said, "It's your turn."

Leontine nodded, deciding she would say it all, as her brave young friend had just showed her to do. She said, "You know how Vincent's mom was sick when we were there? Well, she's really scared, and she told me some things from the past that made me feel afraid. She's even sicker now, and I'm afraid I'll never know enough about what she told me to be able to make anything better. Plus, Carlito is all alone at the ranch now, and they might have to sell it because there's no one to take care of it. He'll lose his home."

Patrick nodded his understanding.

"And you know that baby that Margarita has? She says it belongs to Mrs. Fordyce, but it's really hers and she wants to keep it, but Mrs. Fordyce wants to try to take him from her. She also wants people to think it was Justito that hurt her husband. Victoria is really afraid she might be able to do both."

"Is that what my dad was talking about?"

"Yes. For some reason I think he's on Mrs. Fordyce's side." Then a few moments of silence followed by, "And now Daisy's brother wants to take her back to San Francisco and I'm afraid she might go. Her younger sisters don't have anyone to take care of them."

"Too bad they can't move in with Carlito," Patrick said.

Leontine's face lit up immediately. She turned in her chair to face Patrick, then she threw both arms around him.

"Patrick! You're brilliant!"

Patrick wasn't exactly sure what had suddenly made Leontine so happy, but he caught the spirit immediately. They had been outside talking for quite some time, and when they got back to their table it was to find Nicholas and Daisy finishing their second cocktail. They were both a little snockered. When Leontine told them of Patrick's suggestion, that the Merrie siblings move onto the rancho with Juan Carlos, all of the animosity from earlier evaporated. Patrick and Leontine ate the chocolate cake together and giggled at the tipsy silliness of the other two while they plotted and planned how a move like that could be accomplished and what the Merrie siblings might do, once arrived. They forgot all about Robert Lovell and Caroline Fordyce dining two tables away.

Topics of conversation at that table had actually been fairly benign, and it was not until they sat with a glass of sherry after the meal was finished that Caroline attempted to steer things in a different direction. It was vitally important that she be well-positioned before the contents of Francis' will became public, and she had concluded advice might come best from someone unencumbered by feelings of loyalty for her late husband.

"Mr. Lovell," she began, "I know you and Francis were not on friendly terms. You must wonder at my desire to meet."

In fact, Lovell had wondered, and even experienced a brief moment of anxiety that she suspected he was complicit in the death of her husband. "I am at your service, Mrs. Fordyce, whatever the reason," he said.

"There is a situation left hanging. If still unresolved when the will is read, I fear I might find myself out in the cold."

"I'll advise you if I am able, of course."

"I have unsigned documents that support my position. I wonder if their very existence is any help to me at all."

"Estate law is complex. I could recommend someone to advise you if that's what you're asking."

"I don't think there's time for that."

"Then if time is a factor, may I suggest you just tell me what you have and what it is you hope to accomplish?"

Caroline sighed, leaned back and took a sip of her sherry. The man was impossible to read. She had hoped it would be clear by the end of the meal whether Lovell would best be approached through vulnerability, adulation, competence or something else entirely. Apparently, this was a different breed of man. She could alter her comportment as easily as changing her dress, but with no clear vision of how to present herself to him most effectively, she was at a loss how to proceed. She did not notice that this rumination was occurring as she looked directly into Robert Lovell's eyes all the while.

"I find that truth rarely requires contemplation, Mrs. Fordyce. You will do us both a disservice if you choose another course."

Caroline smiled, the path now revealed as truth. "I was contemplating, Mr. Lovell, the most effective means to manipulate you."

Lovell smiled in return, charmed. "And what did you come up with?"

Caroline felt free then, to lay out the entire situation: the wills, the adoption papers and even her trepidation that she might find life with Margaret Ramirez and her son so bothersome that, in the end, it would not have been worth all the effort.

Lovell had never met a woman so secure in her own motivations. He found it refreshing, and looked for a reason to extend their association.

"A case could be mounted that your husband's intentions had changed based on the evidence of the new will," he said.

"And I could live as I have been while the case went on?"

"That could be the request to the court."

"And mother and child could remain in Santa Barbara, out from underfoot?"

"Unless you fought for custody. It could drag on for years, though you would no doubt lose in the end. Who knows what new opportunities might present in the meantime," Lovell said with undisguised insinuation.

Caroline smiled again. How short-sighted she had been. Francis Fordyce was far from the only middle-aged man of means to grasp at a second chance when mired in the consequences of his life's choices.

"I must ask you, Mr. Lovell, if you know what happened to Francis on Thursday night," Caroline said.

"I decline to answer at the moment. We could meet again – say dinner tomorrow – and perhaps I'll tell you then." He raised his glass to her and Caroline raised hers in return.

Everything might work out just fine.

CHAPTER 21
Thursday, August 26th

✦

The Birabent Market was devoid of customers on this Thursday morning, providing a long-awaited opportunity for quiet conversation with Uncle Remy. Leontine prepared two cups of coffee and carried them to the front of the store. With a smile, Remy dog-eared the page in his book, then dragged his stool over to the counter to face Leontine seated on her stool on the other side.

They chatted idly for a few minutes, then Leontine finally ventured, "Uncle Remy, have you ever heard anything about Vincent having an older brother?"

"Yeah," Remy said, then looked away and took a sip of his coffee.

"Did you know him?"

"I knew who he was." Remy looked at her then, but did not elaborate.

"Innocencia told me some things about him and Vincent's father and a horrible story about a stolen treasure." Uncle Remy nodded his head, which she took to mean he knew the story, too.

"Was Juan Pablo a bad man?"

"Let's just say no one was ever sorry to see the back of him."

"She made it sound as though he killed people, or anyway that they died because of him," Leontine said, leaving out Innocencia's own perceived guilt.

"She's talking about some bad business that went on all around Ortega Ridge. He disappeared after that. For good."

"When?"

"Early eighties, about."

"Before I was born."

"Long before. I don't guess there's much good in dusting it off now."

Leontine sighed, thinking he was no doubt right about that. She finished her coffee and got to her feet. "I'm meeting Daisy at the Western

Union office to send a message to Vincent's sister. Then I'm going to Victoria's to get her birthday present," she said. "I hope you're coming to the party."

"Wouldn't miss it," he replied, then dragged his stool back to his reading corner as Leontine left to meet Daisy.

Further up State Street at the Edison office, E. J. Stambach sat sulking at his desk. Much earlier, unable to sleep, he had tossed and turned in the dark, attempting to calculate the depth of his financial disaster again and again in his mind. He would never be able to rest until he saw the numbers in black and white, so he finally slipped from his bed and dressed as quietly as possible so as not to disturb his sleeping wife and children. Less than half an hour later, he sat at his desk staring at the accounts ledger. It showed clearly that, however worrisome the situation in Hope Ranch might be, he had no choice but to finish the job. Removing the transformer and disappearing from the project had been a mistake, and he hoped he would be able to smooth things over with Patillo.

E. J. stood from the desk with a sigh. If he got moving now, he might be able to re-connect the equipment before the rest of the workmen arrived. He put on his hat and coat, then stood staring at the floor, still wracked with indecision, until he heard someone come in the front door. He wondered who could possibly have business this early in the morning and why he had not thought to lock the door.

Stepping into the main office, he found Robert Lovell, a large envelope clasped behind his back, studying an electrical diagram of the Potter Theater that hung on the office wall as art. Lovell turned when he heard E. J. enter and smiled broadly.

"Good morning, Mr. Stambach. I'm glad I caught you."

"Good morning."

Lovell extended the envelope in E. J.'s direction saying, "I should apologize. They told me you pulled your equipment and left the job yesterday. I can only assume it's because I have been slow to complete our agreement."

E. J. put his hands in his pockets. Lovell lowered the envelope and his eyes narrowed.

"I'm not an idiot," E. J. said.

"I'm not sure what you mean."

"Two weeks ago, you asked me if there was any way a person could get killed on the trolley car, and then a man turns up dead in the exact same way I said. I think I can add two and two."

Lovell extended the envelope once more saying, "I'm sure you can, but I think you need to see this."

E. J. looked away. It was all he could do to resist reaching for the envelope.

"We can help or hurt each other, Mr. Stambach. I hope you won't chose the latter."

"Is that a threat?"

"An appeal to reason." Lovell kept his eyes on E. J.'s face and the transparent display of his internal tug-of-war. A full minute went by before he continued, saying, "Is the decision really so difficult? Something is always better than nothing."

E. J. took the envelope then, and Lovell smiled. "The carbonated copy is for you, but please sign them both."

"I didn't say I was signing it."

"You can have them delivered to me once it's done."

Faced with Lovell's arrogance, E. J.'s temper got the better of him again, and he tossed the envelope back to Lovell who caught it in surprise.

"Forget it," E. J. said, "I'd rather be ruined than work for a killer. Now get out of my office." E. J. stood ramrod straight, deeply aware that he had just accused a very powerful man of being a murderer. He regretted it instantly.

Lovell read the alarm in E. J.'s expression, and allowed himself an indulgent smirk. He said, "I don't see much future for this little project in Hope Ranch. Certainly nothing a man could base his livelihood on. You're probably not aware of this, but the railroad employs many electricians in its own right. A stable position with a large company can be a godsend for a man with a family."

"You don't know anything about me."

"Los Angeles is growing so fast - such a great opportunity to get ahead. I can help you. Please don't doubt that."

E. J. rubbed his eyes, returned to his desk and sank onto his chair. His look fell to his accounts ledger and he leaned forward, holding his head in his hands.

"You'll receive an offer from Southern Pacific before the end of the work day tomorrow. I think you'll love Los Angeles."

E. J. kept his eyes on his desk as Lovell turned to leave. When the lawyer reached to open the door E. J. asked, "Why did you do it?"

"I don't know what you're talking about," Lovell replied without turning around, then he stepped outside.

Leontine and Daisy arrived at the Western Union office with the telegram they had composed the evening before, putting forth the proposal in the briefest of terms, that Will and his sisters be allowed to move into the Barón family farmhouse with Juan Carlos. They asked for a return telegram stating if the sisters were at all receptive to the idea, and if they would be willing to meet with Daisy in person to discuss the notion further.

Once the telegram was dispatched, Leontine walked with Daisy the remaining block to the *Independent*, planning to then catch the trolley back to lower State to head over to Victoria's. Just as they approached the newspaper office, E. J. emerged from his office. He turned to lock the door, so engrossed in his financial woes he failed to notice anything else. He strode quickly up State Street, ahead of the women, in the direction of the Stanwood Livery Stable on East Victoria where he kept his horse. As he walked, the morning sun shone through his bushy blonde hair, and Daisy and Leontine shared a look of surprise – each of them recognizing him as the man who had been watching them from the cliff above Castle Rock as they searched for clues. It was too great an opportunity to let pass.

"Excuse me!" Daisy called out, but he kept walking.

"Excuse me! Please – Edison Company! Sir!" At that, he did turn around, and Daisy and Leontine quickened their pace to catch up with him. As they approached, E. J. recognized them as the women he had seen on the beach, and Daisy as the reporter from the newspaper office next door to his own. He tipped his hat to them and said, "Good morning."

Leontine and Daisy shared another glance, wordlessly agreeing that Daisy would take the lead.

"I'm your neighbor – from the *Independent*," Daisy said as she waved an arm in the general direction of the office. "Daisy Merrie, and this is my friend, Miss Birabent."

E. J. fully removed his hat and dipped his head in greeting.

"Forgive me for asking, but were you down by Castle Rock last Friday?"

"Friday?"

"Up on the bluffs? By the Leadbetter Mansion?"

"I – I - Why do you ask?"

"I'm sorry. I'm being rude. It's just that – we thought we saw you. It was right after they found that dead man."

E. J. couldn't think of a reason to lie. "Yes, it was me."

"Did you know Francis Fordyce?"

"Not really. He hired me is all."

"How did you know he was there?"

"I didn't. I mean – I got wind of the body like everyone else, but I didn't know who it was." E. J. turned his head toward Victoria Street, hoping the women would understand he had someplace else to be.

"Just curiosity then."

"You could say that."

A pause ensued that stretched on long enough for Leontine to recognize they were about to lose him. They needed to get to the point in a hurry. She asked, "What made you suspect the victim had something to do with Hope Ranch? The hat?"

E. J.'s expression betrayed his surprise. He wasn't sure what these two were up to, but he did know one thing: they were not the enemy. "Yes," he admitted. "The hat - and some other things."

"And you left it at the bar for Mr. Reed?" Daisy asked.

"I did."

"What did you want him to know?"

"Nothing. I mean, I just thought it could help."

"Help who?"

"I don't know. I just knew it needed looking into."

"Please, Mr. – " Leontine paused, not having learned his name.

"Stambach."

"Mr. Stambach, I wonder if you would consider talking with the sheriff. Your suspicions could prove useful."

E. J. thought it over. Lovell had made it clear there was no grand future for him with the trackless trolley, but he would be damned if he'd move to Los Angeles and work for the devil himself. The more he thought about it, the more it made sense to throw his lot in with the local law. He didn't have much faith the sheriff would be able to take down someone so rich and powerful, but at least the whole thing would be off his own chest and he could get back to digging up business the usual way.

"Would you like us to go with you? We're quite good friends of Sheriff Stewart," Leontine offered.

"Yes, all right," E. J. said, then squared his shoulders, resolving to tell his whole tale.

Half an hour more, and the three sat together in Nat Stewart's office.

"How do you know it wasn't an accident?" the lawman asked.

"The pole that can be pulled away from the overhead wire was connected, and the lights and controller and everything inside the car were shut off. For him to get electrocuted, something in the car had to have been on and the pole pulled away from the wire. Someone had to re-attach it and turn everything off after he was killed."

"What makes you think it was Lovell?"

"He asked me a week before if there was any danger that someone could get electrocuted in a trolley car. Like a fool, I told him how. I thought he was worried about the safety of the passengers."

Daisy said, "This is the third person pointing a finger at Lovell, but I sure don't see how you prove a thing like this. Not without a witness."

"Or a confession," said Leontine.

"I doubt I'll get that," said the sheriff, "but I definitely need to have a conversation with Mr. Lovell."

CHAPTER 22

Once Sheriff Stewart had the lay of the land, he wasted no time in making his way to the Potter Hotel to seek out Lovell.

When he inquired at the front desk, he learned that the lawyer had checked out of the hotel earlier that morning. He thanked the desk clerk, then proceeded to stand there drumming his fingers and staring into the distance as he decided what to do next. The clerk said, "You might find him at the train station, Sheriff. That's where the porter sent his bags."

"Much obliged." Stewart tipped his hat to the young man, then headed back through the lobby, out the front entrance and around to the side gate that lead directly to the railroad station.

Several hotel employees were working feverishly to clean and re-stock one of two Pullman cars parked on the railroad siding next to the station. It was fairly common to find the luxurious train cars parked behind the hotel, some of which were owned by the railroad for well-heeled travelers willing to pay the price to rent them, and some owned outright by the riders themselves and attached to the train for a substantial fee. Though the sheriff had been peripherally aware of the Pullman cars, he'd not had occasion to look inside one before. He was pretty sure a man like Lovell would settle for nothing less, so he walked to the back of the one with all the activity, mounted the steps up to a little porch and poked his head inside.

Stewart expected it to be fancy, but could never have imagined the extent of the extravagance. The staff was just finishing the preparations, and though the day was growing warm, it was cool inside the Pullman car. Thick curtains of forest-green velvet with braided gold trim covered the windows, shielding the interior from weather and the commotion of the busy station. Electric lights glowed from a coffered ceiling, an electric-lit chandelier hanging in the center. Rich wood paneling extended down the walls of the surprisingly spacious interior. On one side of the car a settee and matching over-stuffed wing-backed chair, upholstered in a plush burgundy-red corduroy fabric, flanked a carved walnut table, upon which rested a silver tray and tea service. Along the opposing bank of windows was a gold brocade chaise lounge next to a marble-topped circular table with a shaded lamp for reading, and a crystal vase of fresh flowers. A lush Persian wool carpet woven into an intricately detailed pattern in deep greens, reds and blues made the coziness of the space complete, and the sheriff would have liked nothing more than to relax into one of the chairs with a good book.

Stewart left the train car and headed for the west wing of the station where horses and carriages delivered travelers with their satchels, bags and steamer trunks for porters to load into storage cars. Half-a-dozen newspaper boys in knickers, suspenders and flat caps hawked their papers, shouting headlines into the general atmosphere. He passed the entrance to the station interior where travelers queued up for tickets, and the east-wing covered patio that included a small fireplace and oak benches where one could wait sheltered from the weather. It was in the exterior receiving area that he found Lovell at last. He was deeply engrossed in a report in the *Los Angeles Herald* about Ned Harriman's return to the states from Austria where he had travelled for his health, when the sheriff stopped in front of him.

"Mr. Lovell?"

Lovell lowered his paper with a scowl, which only deepened when he saw the sheriff's badge. "Yes?"

Stewart was going to sit beside him on the bench seat, then decided he preferred to loom over him. "I just had a talk with Mr. Stambach."

"I'm sorry, I'm not acquainted."

"He runs an electric company here in town. You've met."

"I see," Lovell said. He folded his paper and laid it on the bench beside him. When he stood to face the sheriff, Stewart saw his attention momentarily pulled to something behind him. He followed his gaze just in time to see Caroline Fordyce disappear into the coziness of the Pullman. When he turned back, Lovell met his look evenly, neither man verbally acknowledging the sight.

"Actually, more than one man has pointed me in your direction. I have the problem of your dead associate, as you know."

"It's a problem for many of us, Sheriff."

"It sure would be better for me if you stayed another day or two."

Lovell turned to retrieve the newspaper displaying the headline announcing the return of Ned Harriman. "Sadly, I'm needed elsewhere. Is there something I can do for you before I go?"

"I'd like to hear you tell me about how Francis Fordyce died."

"Then I'm afraid I can't help you."

"I don't want to make it an official request."

"You couldn't possibly."

Lovell bent to pick up a leather case near his feet. He straightened, saying, "Contact my office if you want to schedule an interview in Los Angeles. Other than that, there's not much I can do." With that, Robert Lovell tipped his hat, then stepped around the sheriff and walked in the direction of the Pullman car.

Sheriff Stewart watched him go. He would make that appointment, but knew also that it wouldn't take long before the day to day business of law enforcement pushed the whole unfortunate incident at Castle Rock farther and farther into the background. It wasn't the first time he'd had to make peace with injustice, and he well knew it would not be the last. With a heavy sigh of resignation, he went to get Lois and return to his office.

When Leontine arrived at Rancheria Street, it was to find Victoria at her tiled table completing the hand embroidery around the hem of the second of Daisy's two new work skirts, commissioned by Leontine. The women held the completed garment up between them, and Leontine gushed at the exquisiteness of the finished product. She pulled out a blank notebook, appropriated from Daisy's store of them tucked underneath her bed, and slid it into a precisely measured hidden side pocket that Victoria had cleverly sewn into a seam. It fit perfectly. Leontine held the garment up to her own body to get an idea of how it would hang with its secret passenger on board.

The door to Victoria's studio was open and they could hear Frankie inside experimenting with his vocal cords, his mother mimicking the sound to encourage him to do it some more. It was a joyful sound and they laughed out loud to hear it.

"May I ask how things stand with Frankie?" Leontine said.

Victoria grinned, saying, "The lady says Margarita will hear from a lawyer, but Margarita does not think so. She says she would never leave unless she already has whatever she wants."

"I have to agree. Will Margarita stay in Santa Barbara?"

"If Jesus keeps up with his work, I say yes," Victoria said, then sat back down to finish her embroidery. Leontine went inside to be entertained by the baby and visit with Margarita until the stitching was finished and she could take the gift home to wrap.

Patrick spent the morning finishing up Daisy's birthday present. He had purchased a Parker pen at Faulding's Book Store with some financial assistance from his father. The slender gilded fountain pen, with eye-dropper filler, curved gold nib and crisp engraved floral pattern, lay on a bed of black velvet inside a wooden case decorated with a painted design matching that of the pen inside. Patrick was carefully carving Daisy's name onto the bottom of the case.

When the task was complete, he stepped outside and whistled for Tesla. He didn't want to think too much in advance about what he intended to do next. He walked toward the shore with frequent stops to toss sticks for Tesla along the way. When he finally reached the Plaza, he continued past the fountain to the edge of the open area where he could see Castle Rock. It looked pretty normal from where he was standing. Tesla tore around the landscaped perimeter of the Plaza, across the sand and into the surf as quick as lightning, then bounded out of the water and headed back to Patrick, stopping momentarily to grab a little-bit-too-large piece of driftwood in his mouth and hopefully, resume their game of fetch.

With a last sidelong look at Castle Rock, Patrick took a breath, then ran to Tesla and wrestled the stick from his mouth. Two minutes more and he was up to his knees in the water himself. He couldn't wait to tell Lulubelle. She would be proud.

At five o'clock Leontine, Patrick, Nicholas and Uncle Remy walked up to the *Daily Independent* at a leisurely pace. When they entered the newspaper office, Leontine was greeted with a cheer which caused her to blush ferociously until she had to turn her face away.

Someone had made a streamer from raw newspaper stock that stretched nearly the width of the room and read "Happy Birthday Daisy and Leontine" in the boldest type face available. There was enough cake and Hires Root Beer laid out to satisfy an army. Victoria, Margarita and the baby were already there talking with Diego who had walked up from the Tally Ho. Daisy's co-workers - including Owen Reed - and a few of the regular customers from the market made up the rest of the group, along with Sheriff Stewart, of course, and even his wife, Mary. It seemed everyone was speaking at once.

Leontine strained to hear Owen Reed informing Daisy that Patillo came by to tell him he had been hired by the Pacific Improvement Company to de-construct the prototype, and of his intention to share the monumental task with E. J. Stambach. Reed then inquired about John Tade, and learned that he had concluded Santa Barbara was ripe for an automobile dealership. He was returning to Los Angeles to learn how to start one up and swore he'd be back very soon.

Leontine joined Patrick in a generous serving of birthday cake, then the two sought out Daisy, her presents hidden behind their backs. Everyone stopped to watch as they gleefully revealed first the clever and exceedingly useful work skirts, then the stylish personalized ink pen.

Daisy presented her dear friend and landlady with her gift then, and looked on with anticipation as Leontine carefully removed the wrapping paper. It was a photograph taken the day the Birabent Market opened that Daisy had found in an archive file titled "State Street Buildings"- though it was not the one that had appeared in the paper at the time. It showed Leontine as a toddler, peeking shyly from behind her mother's skirt. Her mother and father and Uncle Remy were smiling and looking down at her, attempting to coax her into the foreground, her mother's hand resting gently on the top of her head. Leontine could not remember ever feeling an affectionate touch from her mother's hand nor a time when she had felt her smile. Yet here was evidence of both in black and white, surrounded by a beautiful silver embossed frame. She passed the photo to Uncle Remy and their eyes met, each blinking back tears.

As was anticipated, the more ardent revelers disappeared in short order and followed Owen Reed to the Stafford Saloon to continue the celebration, Daisy among them. Most went on home and strolled up or down State Street toward their various dwellings. Patrick and Nicholas walked Leontine to her door, parting with heartfelt hugs and well wishes.

In the quiet of her apartment, Leontine placed the photograph on her mantle alongside the carved dove and an engraved bell – a gift from her father. Her heart expanded, and she named for herself her most cherished gifts; the love she felt for her family and friends and the safety and security of her home.

It was the best birthday she'd ever had.

Annie J. Dahlgren

Through the years, Annie has earned many awards and much recognition as a writer, director, producer, editor and performer. Four CDs of her original music can be found on all major music streaming sites, and are available for purchase through iTunes, Amazon and most well-known websites where music is sold.

A YouTube search using her name or that of her production company, Over 40 Productions, will yield dozens of music videos and short films that are written, produced, directed and/or edited by Annie. A feature film of her story The Bet won the La Femme Film Festival in Los Angeles in 2014 and hopefully, one day, will find its way to distribution.

Now focused on the "Santa Barbara History Mysteries" series of novels, along with writing partner Neal Graffy, these stories follow events in the lives of Leontine Birabent and her friends Patrick and Daisy. The novels intend to provide a genuine sense of what life was like in the beautiful city of Santa Barbara during the early 20th century,

---

OTHER PROJECTS by Annie J. Dahlgren

Music CDs
Available on iTunes, CD Baby, anniejdahlgren.com

Fortunes Made
A Better Life
All Through the Night
Alley Cat

Feature Film
The Bet (co-writer)

Audio Plays
Fortunes Made

Musical Theater
Moment of Truth
(book)

Award-winning Screenplays
Sisters of Mercy
Too Tall Townsend

Deceivers (co-writer)
The Bet
Spirit Guides
Vigilance
New Texacornia

Music Video Productions
YouTube: Search on "Over 40 Productions"

Contact Annie at www.anniejdahlgren.com

Neal Graffy

"Delightfully unfettered by convention" pretty much sums up Neal Graffy's approach to history. Whether it be in print, radio, television, documentary or live, his audiences always find his presentations to be entertaining, fun and still educational.

Neal first gave voice to history in 1989 when he premiered a slide show talk on Santa Barbara History. Encouraged by the response, more talks were developed; and currently there are twenty different topics that have been presented in well over 250 shows.

Expanding from solo presentations, Graffy has had numerous appearances on local, state and national radio and TV including Huell Howser's *California's Gold*, KCET TV's *Life and Times* and nationally on *This Old House*. He has been featured in several documentaries including the Emmy Award winning *Impressions in Time*.

In addition to books on Santa Barbara history, he has authored numerous monographs for historical organizations, as well as articles in regional and national publications.

For fun, he collects Santa Barbara memorabilia and postcards, photographs, plays guitar, plus enjoys cruising around town in his unrestored 1941 Packard 180 limousine.

OTHER PROJECTS by Neal Graffy

Current Publications
Santa Barbara Then & Now
Street Names of Santa Barbara
Historic Santa Barbara

Forthcoming Publications
The Great Santa Barbara Earthquake -
  The Disaster that Built a City
Santa Barbara's Grand Hotel – The Potter
History Under Your Nose

A Partial List of Lectures
A Liar, A Drunk and a Piano Teacher -
  The Story of the Flying 'A' Studios
Santa Barbara's Grand Hotel - The Potter
Santa Barbara Then & Now
Montecito's Hilltop Barons
The Great Santa Barbara Earthquake –
  The Disaster That Built a City

Street Names of Santa Barbara
Two Hotels and a Theater - The Story
  of the Arlington
History Under Your Nose
Fiestas, Festivals and Parades --
  Santa Barbara Celebrates!
Naples - A Tale of Two Cities
Santa Barbara's Powerful Women
A History of Mission Canyon
Fremont, Foxen & the San Marcos Pass
Norton I - The Forgotten Emperor
  of the United States
E Clampus Vitus – No Known Cure
Goleta – In Search of History
Santa Barbara – The Search for Water
Santa Barbara Adobes
Why Santa Barbara?

Contact Neal at www.elbarbareno.com

Coming next:

Ortega Ridge

Remy said, "She's talking about some bad business that went on all around Ortega Ridge. Juan Pablo left after that. For good."